"Something tells me that down deep, you don't agree with what you have to believe."

Her touch spilled heat into Zac's gut. He was no saint, but he could honestly say he hadn't felt that kind of fire in a long time. Whether it was wishful thinking or plain wanting action, he didn't know, but he liked it. Given his current status as the prosecutor on her brother's case, thinking like that would lead him nowhere good.

Emma snatched her finger back. He smiled and her cheeks immediately flushed. Too damned cute. Even if he should be running like hell.

"I need to go," she said.

For safety, Zac stepped far enough out of reach so he didn't do something stupid and touch her. "Yes, you do."

The Prosecutor

ADRIENNE GIORDANO

First published in Great Britain 2014
by Mills & Boon, an imprint of Harlequin (UK) Limited,
Large Print edition 2014
Eton House, 18-24 Paradise Road,
Richmond, Surrey, TW9 1SR

© 2014 Adrienne Giordano

ISBN: 978 0 263 24449 6

ADRIENNE GIORDANO

USA TODAY bestselling author Adrienne Giordano writes romantic suspense and mystery. She is a Jersey girl at heart, but now lives in the Midwest with her workaholic husband, sports-obsessed son and Buddy the Wheaten Terrorist (Terrier). She is a cofounder of Romance University blog and Lady Jane's Salon-Naperville, a reading series dedicated to romantic fiction.

Adrienne decided to write *The Prosecutor* after seeing a news segment on a wrongly convicted man. For more information on *The Defender*, Adrienne's next Mills & Boon® Intrigue book, please visit www.adriennegiordano.com. Adrienne can also be found on Facebook, at www.facebook.com/ AdrienneGiordanoAuthor, and on Twitter, at www.twitter.com/ AdriennGiordano. For information on Adrienne's street team, Dangerous Darlings, go to www.facebook.com/ groups/DangerousDarlings

For Elisa and Chris, who make the complexities of sibling relationships easy to navigate. I love you.

Chapter One

Assistant State's Attorney Zac Hennings leaned back in his chair the second before a newspaper smacked against his desk.

"If there's any blowback on this," Ray Gardner said, "it's yours."

Zac glanced at the newspaper. On page one, below the fold, was a photo of a young woman—*brunette*—gazing out a window framed by a set of gold drapes. Someone's living room. The headline read Fighting for Justice. He skimmed the first few paragraphs. The Chelsea Moore murder.

A burst of adrenaline exploded in Zac's brain. *Big case.*

Turning from the newspaper, he looked back to

his boss. Ray's generic gray suit fit better than most he wore but still hung loose on his lean frame. Once in a while, to keep his staff sharp, Ray would show up in a blue or black suit. Regardless, the guy needed a good tailor, but Zac wasn't going to be the one to suggest it. Not when Ray led the Criminal Prosecutions Bureau, the largest of the six divisions of the Cook County State's Attorney's Office.

Ray gestured to the newspaper. "The Sinclairs got traction with this. Steve Bennett—"

"The detective? The one who died last week?"

"That's him. Brain cancer. He apparently refused to face his maker without clearing his conscience. He sent Emma Sinclair a video—starring himself— telling her the witness who ID'ed her brother wasn't sure he got the right guy. According to Steve, detectives pressured the witness into saying he was positive."

Zac took his time with that one, let it sink in. "We locked up Brian Sinclair for murder and now we've got deathbed revelations?"

"Something like that. The State's Attorney called me at six this morning after seeing her newspaper. She wants the office bulldog on this. That's you, by the way. You'll have all the case files this afternoon."

More files. Every open space in Zac's office had been jammed with stacks of folders containing all the lurid details of crimes ranging from robberies to murders. Where he'd put more files he had no idea, but as one of nine hundred assistant prosecutors in Chicago, a city plagued with over five hundred murders last year, he had bigger problems than storage space.

Not for the first time, his responsibilities settled at the base of his neck. He breathed in, gave that bit of tension its due diligence and put it out of his mind. Unlike some of the attorneys around him, he lived for moments like this. Moments when that hot rush of scoring an important case made him "the man," marching into court, going to battle and kicking some tail.

The cases were often brutal, not to mention

emotionally paralyzing, but his goal would always be telling the victim's loved ones they got a guilty verdict. No exceptions. In this case, they'd already convicted someone. Zac had to make it stick.

Adding to the drama was Chelsea's father, Dave, who was a veteran Chicago homicide detective. A good, honest cop who'd lost his child to a senseless act of violence.

In short, Zac wanted to win.

Every time.

"We're already behind the curve with this article," Ray said.

"I'll get us caught up."

When Chelsea Moore's murder occurred, Zac had been grinding his way through misdemeanors. After getting promoted to felonies, he'd worked like a dog to win his cases and it paid off. Big-time. Ray had just assigned him a politically and emotionally volatile case that he'd bleed for in order to keep Chelsea's killer behind bars.

No matter how hard Emma Sinclair came at

them, Dave's daughter deserved justice. And Zac would see that she got it. He'd study the trial transcripts and learn the facts of the case.

"The P.D. will go to the wall for Dave Moore," Ray said.

"Yep. The guy breaks cases no one else can. He won't tolerate his daughter's murderer going free. His buddies won't, either."

Ray pointed. "Bingo."

If Emma Sinclair managed to get her brother's conviction overturned, the Chicago P.D. would not only be angry, they'd also make sure Helen Jergins, the new State's Attorney who'd promoted Zac, got run out of town. Hard.

Ray shifted toward the door then turned back. "Whatever you need, you let me know. We have to win this one."

"I got this," Zac said. "Count on it."

EMMA STOOD IN FRONT of the huge whiteboard she'd rolled to her mother's basement wall and contemplated her revised list of target defense attorneys. Given the newspaper article, today would be the day to once again get cracking on Project Sinclair.

Eighteen months ago her twenty-two-year-old brother, a guy who had nothing but love for those around him, had been convicted of strangling a young woman outside a nightclub. Unable to withstand the injustice of the circumstantial case—no fingerprints or DNA—Emma started banging on the doors of defense attorneys all over the city, trying to win a reversal. No matter how many times she was told no, she would not be silenced. Not when her innocent brother was rotting in prison.

She flicked her finger against the whiteboard. The new video evidence would lure one of these lawyers in. It had to. The case suddenly had all the political melodrama—corruption, false witness testimony, withholding information—defense attorneys thrived on.

She spun back to the oblong folding table, shoved aside an open banker's box, grabbed the binder with her latest set of research and made a note to study up on *Brady* and *Giglio* material. Being a first-year law student, a field she'd never imagined for herself, she hadn't yet mastered the concepts, but they involved impeaching a witness and items prosecutors were required to share with the defense. Maybe in the next few days she'd have a defense attorney—preferably pro bono, considering that she was broke—to help her slice through the technical aspects of the case.

Above her head, the exposed water pipe clunked. Her mother flushing the toilet. Emma sighed. She should move all this stuff upstairs to Brian's old room, but her mother didn't need to see a daily reminder that her son was a convicted murderer. Bad enough the poor woman had to think about it, never mind see it every time she walked upstairs.

So Emma and her effort to free her brother would stay in the cold, dreary basement, surrounded by cobwebs that, no matter how many times she brushed them away, kept returning.

When the time came for her to move out on her own again, she'd have a finished basement. No doubt about it. For now, she'd left her cute little apartment in Wrigleyville so her widowed mother wouldn't have to face her demons alone.

A rapid click-click-click of heels hitting the battered hardwood came from the first floor. Emma had spent countless hours listening to her mother's footsteps above. Whether early morning or the darkness of night when sleep eluded them, Emma recognized the sound of her mother's shoes. The ones she'd just heard didn't belong to her mom. *Someone's here.*

"Emma?" her mother called from the doorway.

"Yes?"

"There's a Penny Hennings here to see you."

Emma froze. *Penny Hennings.* She perused her whiteboard, where she'd alphabetized the lawyers' names. Hennings. There it was. Not Penny, though. Gerald, from Hennings and Solomon.

Maybe Penny was a relative sent to check her out for Gerald Hennings, who might want to take the case. And if said relation fought downtown traffic on a weekday morning and hauled herself to the North Side, to Parkland, it had to be serious. Emma linked her fingers together and squeezed. *Please, let it be.*

"Be right up, Mom."

She glanced down at her sweats, torn T-shirt and pink fuzzy slippers. Great. She'd have to face some snazzy lady from a big-time law firm in this getup. She plucked a rubber band from the little bowl with the paper clips. Least she could do was tie back her tangled hair.

Rotten luck.

Forget it. She had to put her appearance out of her mind. For all she knew, Penny Hennings could be a cosmetics saleswoman.

But what were the chances of that? Particularly at 9:00 a.m. on the morning an article about Brian ran?

"Emma?" her mother called.

"Coming."

She straightened. If Penny Hennings *was* from

Hennings and Solomon, Emma had to go into full sales mode and convince this woman that her firm should take Brian's case. After eighteen months of studying overturned convictions and hounding lawyers, it was time for their odds to change. And Hennings and Solomon could make that happen.

Emma ditched her slippers at the base of the stairs and marched up. She looked like hell, but she'd dazzle this would-be-lawyer-slash-cosmetics-saleswoman with her powers of persuasion.

The basement door stood open and Mom's voice carried from the living room. Emma closed her eyes. *This could be it.* After a long, streaming breath, she stepped out of the short hallway.

A minuscule woman—maybe late twenties—with shoulder-length blond hair sat on the sofa. The plaid, overstuffed chair tried to swallow her, but her red power suit refused to be smothered. No, that puppy screamed strength and defiance and promise. Could be a good sign.

Plus, to the woman's credit, she kept her gaze on

Emma's face and not her attire. One cool cookie, this blonde.

Emma extended her hand to the now standing woman. "Hello. I'm Emma Sinclair."

"Good morning. I'm Penny Hennings. I'm an attorney from Hennings and Solomon. I'm sorry to barge in, but I saw the story on your brother this morning."

Emma glanced at her mother, took in her cloudy, drooping brown eyes and flat mouth. A heavy heart had stolen her mother's joy. Ten years ago, at the age of forty, the woman had been widowed and learned that hope could be a fickle thing. Emma, though, couldn't give in to that defeatist thinking. There was a reason she'd been left fatherless at sixteen and now, with her brother in prison, had assumed the role her father would want her to take. To watch over Mom and free Brian.

Some would say she didn't deserve all this loss. Why not? It turned out their family had crummy luck. Her father's sudden death from a brain aneurysm had left a void so deep she'd never really acknowledged it for fear that she'd be consumed by it and would cease experiencing the joy the world offered. Ignoring that vast hole inside her seemed easier.

Then Brian went to prison—more crummy luck—and the hole inside grew. The thing she held on to day after day, the thing that kept her focused and sane and standing, was the fight to free her brother.

Whatever it took, she'd find a way to put their family back together.

"Ms. Sinclair?"

Make this happen. "Forgive me. I'm…well, I'm trying not to get ahead of myself, but you're the first attorney to contact me in eighteen months and I'm really, *really* happy to see you."

Penny offered a wide smile and instantly Emma's pulse settled. "Please, have a seat. Would you like coffee?"

"No, thank you. I can't stay long. I spoke to my father—Gerald Hennings—on the way over. He indicated that you'd contacted him about this case some months back."

Emma sat on the love seat and rested her hand over her mother's. Maybe they'd finally get the break they deserved. "Yes. He was kind enough to review the case, but said there was nothing he could do."

"At the time, that was true, but I'm intrigued by this video you've obtained. If the video is accurate, we might be able to prove that your brother's constitutional rights were violated. Any information regarding witness testimony should have been turned over to the defense before trial."

"It's *Giglio* material, right?" Emma asked.

Penny cocked her head. "You've brushed up."

"Yes. I'm also a first-year law student at Northwestern. I left a job at a public relations firm so I'd be available during the day to work on my brother's case. With the hands-on experience, I figured I might as well go to law school. I waitress at night and work my classes in around everything else."

"Wow. You're good."

Emma shrugged. "Not really. My brother is innocent and he's slated to spend the next twenty-five years in prison. I can't let that happen."

Penny's expression remained neutral, her lips free of any tightening or forced smiles. No pity. Good. They didn't need pity. They needed a shrewd legal rainmaker.

"That's why I'm here. I'd like to review the information you've collected and possibly take your case. Pro bono. I'm not going to lie: this will be tough. The victim's father is a Chicago P.D. detective. The State's Attorney will go to war with us to keep your brother in prison, but I won't back down. If Brian's rights were violated, I'll prove it. Besides that, I'm hungry for a big case and I think yours might just be the one."

Suddenly, Penny Hennings seemed young. Idealistic maybe. Not the battle-hardened defense attorney her father was. Did it matter? Her wanting to step out from under her father's shadow and make a name for herself was a great motivator.

She's a rainmaker, smart and determined.

Emma gestured down the hall to the basement door. "Would you like to see what I have on the case?"

Penny smiled. "You bet I would."

ZAC PUSHED HIS ROlling cart stuffed with case files from the courtroom to his fifth-floor office. Along the way he passed other prosecutors dragging their own heavy loads and their stone faces or smirking, sly grins told the tales of their wins and losses.

Zac's day had consisted of jury selection for a murder trial he was scheduled to prosecute. The pool of candidates wasn't ideal, but his evidence was strong and he'd parlay that into a win.

He nudged the cart through his doorway and turned back to the bull pen for Four O'clock Fun. On most days, prosecutors coming from court gathered to compare notes, discuss the personalities of judges and opposing lawyers, anything that might be good information for one of the other

ASAs. Some days, Four O'clock Fun turned into a stream of stories that would scandalize the average person, but that prosecutors found humorous. For Zac, gallows humor was a form of self-protection. A way to keep his sanity in the face of the day-to-day evil he grappled with.

"Zac," Stew Henry yelled, "Pierson got his butt kicked by Judge Alred today."

"Seriously?"

Alred had to be the easiest-going guy on the bench. It took a lot to aggravate him. Two steps toward the bull pen, Zac's cell phone rang. He checked the screen. Alex Belson, the public defender on the Sinclair case, returning his call.

"Have to take this," Zac yelled to the bull pen before heading back to his office. "Alex, hey, thanks for getting back to me."

"No prob. Got to say, screwy timing since your sister called me today, too."

"My sister?"

What's that about?

"Yeah. She's taking the Sinclair case. Wants copies of all my notes."

Zac dropped into his chair to absorb this info.

"You didn't know?" Alex asked.

Penny had left a voice mail earlier in the day, but he'd been in court and hadn't had a chance to get back to her. "I haven't talked to her today."

Another call beeped in and Zac checked the screen. Penny. "Alex, let me call you back." He flashed over to his sister. "Pen?"

The sound of a horn blasted. Outdoors.

"Hi," she said. "Are you in your office?"

"Yeah."

"I'm walking into the lobby. Be there in two minutes."

She was here. "What's this about your taking the Sinclair case?"

"Word travels fast. How'd you know?"

"The PD told me. Pen, I caught this case."

Silence. *Yeah, little sister, soak that up.* If this case went forward, Zac would be battling his baby sister in court. At twenty-nine, only two years his junior, she was equally competitive when it came to winning her cases. Plus, she had their legendary father as co-counsel.

In short, it would be a bloodbath.

Unfortunately for his sister, Zac planned on winning and giving Dave Moore justice for his daughter.

"So," Pen said, "I guess my calling you to find out who Ray assigned proved fruitful."

"You don't want this case. It's a dog."

"Not a chance, big brother. See you in a minute."

Zac hung up and stared through the open doorway where raucous laughter from Four O'clock Fun raged on. That Alred story must have been a good one. He should have stayed and listened. He could use the laugh.

Two minutes later, Penny swung into his office. Behind her strode a woman wearing tan pants and a black sweater. Emma Sinclair. He'd never met her, but had seen photos of her, including the one from the morning paper still sitting on his desk.

That photo hadn't done Emma any favors. In person, her dark hair extended below her shoulders and, when Zac took in the soft curve of her cheek and her big brown eyes, something in his chest pinged. Just a wicked stinging that reminded him he was in desperate need of a woman's affections.

Except she was his opponent.

Why the hell was Penny bringing her here?

"Hello, *Zachary*," Penny said in that sarcastic, singsong way she'd been addressing him for years. She stepped forward to give him the usual kiss on the cheek, but caught herself.

Yeah, welcome to Awkwardville. For the first time, they were squaring off against each other in the professional arena. Considering that his father and his two siblings were all attorneys, Zac had known he'd eventually face one of them in court. The only thing that had saved him thus far was the Chicago crime rate providing enough cases to go around.

Until now.

Pen gestured to Emma. "Zachary Hennings, meet Emma Sinclair. Brian Sinclair's sister."

Zac stepped around the desk and shook hands with Emma. What he expected, he wasn't sure, but for some reason her warm, firm grip surprised him. Their gazes met for a split second and the intense, deep coffee brown of her eyes nearly knocked him on his butt. But he couldn't think about Emma Sinclair and her alluring eyes and how they affected him. He had to think of Chelsea Moore.

Dead Chelsea Moore.

He released Emma's hand and stooped to clear the files off the second chair in his office. The place was a mess. "Have a seat."

On his way back to his desk, he shot Penny a *what-the-heck?* look. She grinned. She wanted to play, he'd play.

While doing so, he'd also remind his baby sister that he wasn't a guy who liked to lose.

EMMA WATCHED ZACHARY HENNINGS—did he really want people calling him *Zachary?*—head back to his desk while she took the seat he'd cleared for her.

He relaxed back in his desk chair, Mr. Casual. As if she'd believe he could be comfortable with Penny as the attorney on a high-profile case and the sister of the convicted sitting in front of him. He certainly looked the part, though. Then again, he had that yacht-club look about him. His short, precisely combed blond hair and perfect bone structure just added to the patrician image. The only thing slightly ruffled about him was the un-fastened top button on his shirt and his loose tie. The look fit him, however. Country-club rugged.

If she'd met him elsewhere, she'd have steered clear of him. In her experience, men who looked like that were either arrogant and patronizing or ignored her altogether. Being Miss Completely Average, she didn't have the high-maintenance looks men like him went for and that was just fine with her. What she needed was a depend-able, rock-solid man who could roll with the in-sanity of her life.

Something told her Zachary Hennings had no interest in a woman with complications. Maybe that was an unfair judgment, but it wasn't for her to worry about.

"So," Penny said. "Let's talk about this video."

Zachary held up a hand and gave a subtle nudge of his chin in Emma's direction. "Is this appropriate?"

"She's my intern."

Her intern. Funny.

"Say what?"

"She's a law student who knows this case better than anyone. Trust me, in her first year at Northwestern she knows more about the law than the two of us combined did as first years. Suck it up. She's staying."

Obviously amused by his sister's antics, he cracked a wide grin. Emma cut her gaze to Penny, then back to Zachary before biting her lip. Down deep, the warrior in her wanted to join the fray, but watching these two hammer away at each other would be just as much fun.

"You were saying about the video? I need a copy, of course."

"Of course." She pulled her phone, hit the screen a couple of times and stuck it back in her purse. "On its way. I'm planning on filing a PCR." Penny turned to Emma. "Post-conviction relief." Emma nodded and Penny went back to her brother. "A video like this, you know we'll get our hearing based on newly discovered evidence."

He shrugged. "No judge in Cook County will vacate a sentence in the murder of a cop's daughter without something better than that video. And hello? Did the detective not have brain cancer? How do we know disease hadn't brought on hallucinations?"

"Please, *Zachary*. You'll need to try harder than that." Penny stood and adjusted the hem of her jacket. "Anyway, I only stopped to see which lucky prosecutor would face me in court. Now that I know, I'm off to make notes on this new evidence. Better start thinking about the State's reply, big brother. See you at dinner on Saturday." She gave him a finger wave. "Toodles. Love you."

Emma sat speechless as Penny strode from the office. Her attorney was one crazy chick, which might not be a good thing, considering that Brian's freedom rested in her hands. But Penny had something. Maybe it was her brash attitude or her willingness to take a chance on Brian, but whatever it was, Emma liked it. A lot.

From his desk chair, Zachary snorted. "She's nuts. Get used to it."

Emma stood. "Maybe so, but I like her spunk."

"She has plenty of that."

Before she turned for the door, Emma stared down at him. "My brother is innocent."

"He was convicted by a jury of his peers."

"And juries never make mistakes?"

No answer. It didn't matter. "I've studied the evidence," she continued. "The public defender blew this one. I can promise you my brother didn't strangle anyone. I'd know."

According to the prosecution's theory, Brian

had left Magic—the nightclub—to meet the victim in the alley beside it. After he murdered her, apparently using the belt from her jacket, he supposedly went back into the club and partied for another hour.

"Were you with him that night?"

"No. But I know my brother. He stole four dollars from my wallet when he was twelve. An hour later the guilt drove him mad and he confessed."

Zachary shrugged. "He was twelve. He's a man now. People change."

"Not my brother. He was living at home with my mother at the time of the murder. Want to know why?"

"Is it relevant to my case?"

"My brother is in prison. Everything is relevant."

Zachary tapped his fingers on the desk. "I'll bite. Why was he living at home?"

"Because our father died ten years ago and I'd moved out. He didn't want our mother to be alone. He had a good job and could have easily afforded to be on his own, but he couldn't stand the idea of his mother being by herself. That's not a man who commits murder."

Emma stopped talking. The past year had taught her the value of silence. Silence offered that perfect span of time when each person decided who would flinch. She stared down at Zachary Hennings.

A fine-looking man she desperately hoped would flinch.

Finally, he stood. He was a good six inches taller than she was, but she held her ground and kept her head high. "No offense, Ms. Sinclair, but you're far from impartial and the daughter of a good cop is dead. Any one of us, given the right circumstances, has the capability to commit murder."

"Not my brother, Mr. Hennings. You'll see." She turned to leave.

"It's Zac. My father is Mr. Hennings. And I can tell you I'll study the case file. I love to win, but I have no interest in keeping an innocent man in prison. That being said, twelve reasonable people heard evidence and decided his fate. I'm not going to go screaming to the judge that it was a mistake. Prove it to me and we'll take it from there."

Chapter Two

In the beat-up hallway outside Zac's office, Emma spotted Penny waiting for her. The moment she got close, Penny headed for the elevator, the two of them moving at a steady clip.

"I'll get started on the petition," Penny said. "What's your schedule the next couple days?"

"I have a class in the morning and then I work tomorrow night. On Saturday, I work at four, but I have all morning and early afternoon open. Sunday I have to study. What do you need?"

"We need to analyze the video and compare what he says to what we know happened around the time of the murder. There has to be something else that will support our case. I think we'll get our hearing anyway because that video is pretty darn compelling, but it wouldn't hurt to have more."

Emma pushed through the lobby door and a burst of cold, early-April wind blew her hair back. Penny remained unruffled, her hair perfectly intact as she whipped through the doorway. Emma would have loved to be that put together, but she didn't have a sense of fashion so she stuck with the basics of slacks and sweaters. Basics were easy and kept her from looking like a fashion disaster.

Penny stopped on the cement steps of the towering building. Behind them, the early rush of employees leaving for the day funneled by.

"I already have a time line built," Emma said. "I'll go through the video and do a second time line with what the detective says. And, oh, I'll get myself on the list to visit Brian tomorrow. I can squeeze that in before work and show him the two time lines. Maybe he can help."

"Good. Anything that seems off, note it and I'll have one of our investigators check it out."

Investigators. All this time, Emma had been trudging around town, fighting every step of the way, begging every defense lawyer, reporter, blogger, anyone who could help, and finally, finally, someone believed in her. Her breath caught and she smacked a hand against her chest.

Penny drew her eyebrows together, marring her perfect porcelain skin. "You okay?"

Maybe. "You have investigators."

"The firm does, yes."

Months of exhaustive, energy-sapping worry erupted into a stream of hysterical laughter. "*Investigators.*"

Penny's eyes widened. Poor woman must have thought her client was insane. Emma laughed harder and grabbed her lawyer's arms. "I've been alone with this for so long. No one has helped. No one. Even my mother has been too depressed to lend a hand, and now you tell me you have investigators. And it won't cost me anything. You have no idea what that means to me."

Finally, the tears came. A flood of them gushing to the surface and tumbling down her face. God, she was tired. Insanity might not be far behind after all.

Penny stepped an inch closer. "Listen, we've got a long road. I'm good, but we're dealing with the murder of a cop's daughter. We're about to climb Everest with no oxygen. Can you make it?"

Emma nodded. This one she knew for sure. "I've already climbed to ten thousand feet without oxygen. I'm not stopping now."

"Good. Then let's do this. Call me with any updates. I've got to go."

Penny charged down the cement steps and Emma pulled her phone from her jacket pocket. Two missed calls. One from Mom. She dialed. "Hi."

"Hi. You had a call. That Melody. The one Brian was dating."

Brian's old girlfriend—well, she couldn't really be called a girlfriend. Melody, according to Brian, was more like a friend with benefits. The fact that this *friend* had called their house on the day an article ran about Brian could not be a co-incidence. Particularly since Melody, again ac-cording to Brian, had spent a few minutes with him around the time of the murder. He'd left the club and walked Melody to her car around 12:30 a.m. that night. The defense never called Mel-ody as a witness and, with Brian not testifying at trial, Emma assumed this information had been deemed irrelevant. Not that she understood it, but she didn't understand a lot of the nuances about Brian's trial.

"What did she want?" Emma asked her mother.

"I don't know. She started talking, then stopped and said she needed to speak with you."

"Did she leave a number?"

"Yes."

Her mother read off the number and Emma re-peated it to herself. "Got it."

She disconnected and entered the number into

her phone before she forgot it. Pedestrians continued to stream from the building and she moved to the side. Another gust of wind caught her coat and she yanked the zipper up to shield herself from the cold air. Stepping away from the pedestrian traffic, she pressed the TALK button, heard the phone ring and waited for Melody to pick up.

Brian's public defender had been no help when it came to Melody. He'd never even pursued her claims because she couldn't prove that Brian had been with her that night. According to the lawyer, she could be covering for him.

As if a casual friend would risk a perjury charge. *Whatever.*

Emma didn't want to revisit her frustrations with Bri's public defender. Unless she could prove his incompetence, it was best left alone. Instead, she'd remind herself that she now had Hennings and Solomon on her side.

"Melody? It's Emma Sinclair."

"Hi, Emma. Thanks for calling me back."

"Sure. What can I help you with?"

"How's Brian?"

He's in prison. "He's holding up."

"I saw the article in the paper."

"They did a nice job." She wasn't about to give an outsider too much information.

"Is there anything I can do to help? I told the prosecution and the defense lawyer that I'd testify. They never contacted me, even after I gave the detectives the receipt from the parking garage."

Suddenly, all movement around Emma ceased—a huge, jarring halt that caused her body to stiffen. "There was a receipt?"

Breathe. Get loose. Too many hopes had been bludgeoned by the cruelty of injustice and she'd learned to temper her optimism. Whatever this receipt was, it couldn't have been anything stunning or the public defender—she'd hope—would have uncovered it.

"Yes," Melody said. "I used a credit card to pay for the garage. It was one of those machines. You stick the ticket in, put your credit card in the slot and you get another ticket that lets you out of the garage. Brian was with me."

Emma paused a second, let the cold air wash over her while she mentally played find-the-missing-receipt. She'd amassed boxes and boxes of notes on the case and had never heard about a parking receipt. Didn't mean the thing wasn't sitting around somewhere, but she would have remembered seeing it. *If* she'd seen it.

Oh, and she could just hear the prosecutors moaning about how it wouldn't prove that Brian had been with Melody and unless they had solid proof, Melody could be protecting her lover.

"Unfortunately, none of this proves where Brian was at the time. I've hired a new lawyer, though. Can I have her contact you?"

"Yes. I mean, he shouldn't be in jail. He didn't do it."

"I know. I'm not giving up." She gripped the phone tighter. "Thank you for calling, Melody. I appreciate it. I know Brian will, too."

Emma hung up and stared at the phone. Now

she had a receipt to chase down, another lead to work with. People continued to file out of the building, their voices and footsteps clicking against the cement.

4:40.

By the look of the mountain of files in his office, Zac Hennings would probably still be at his desk. He struck her as the diligent type—a man who'd sit and study his notes, losing all track of time. Maybe she'd march up and demand—no—*ask* about the receipt. Playing nice with the new prosecutor might get her a little cooperation.

If not, too bad. She wanted answers.

ALREADY, ZAC HAD determined one thing. The video had to be deep-sixed. On a decent day, a detective's deathbed confession was a nightmare scenario. Couple that with Zac's rabid sister and the persistent Emma Sinclair and he had one hell of a problem. Emma didn't have his sister's flashy clothes and sarcastic manner, but she obviously had a quick mind and adjusted to conflict easily. With these two, he'd have his hands full.

First thing was to obtain copies of all the case files and interview the detectives.

Still at his desk, he tapped the screen again and the dying detective's face appeared. Damn, he looked bad. It could be a major problem in court. Who wouldn't be sympathetic to someone dying of cancer?

He set the phone down and jotted notes as the now-deceased detective spoke. *Witness unsure. Alley dark. Couldn't positively ID. Showed a six-pack*—the old photo lineup where the witness was given photographs of possible suspects and asked if he could identify any of them. In this case, according to the dying detective, the witness *thought* that *maybe* Brian Sinclair *could be* the guy.

All of it should be documented in the case files.

Zac shook his head as the detective confessed to coaxing the witness with leading questions. *He had dark hair, right? And a white shirt, correct?*

Zac studied the detective's sallow face, seeking anything that might indicate that brain cancer had caused mental impairment. Outside of the papery, sagging skin that came with chemo treatments, his speech was clear and he seemed rational. Zac checked the date on the bottom of the screen. Six weeks ago. He'd have to research the effects of brain cancer in the weeks prior to death. To refute this evidence, he'd simply need to prove that the man had lost cognitive brain function. In which case, everything on the video would be thrown out.

Problem solved.

Next. Identification of the white shirt worn by the accused might be something for Penny to run with. The murder happened in March. It could have been cold. Did the assailant wear a jacket? That had to have come up in court.

Again, all this information should be in the case files, which Zac didn't have. He scooped up his desk phone and dialed his office assistant. "Hey,

Beth. Have you seen the files from the Sinclair case yet?"

"I put them in your office. They're in a box by the corner window."

On the floor sat one square file box, maybe eleven by thirteen inches. A corner of the lid was torn, as if someone had tried to lift it and it ripped. "That's it?"

"That's all that was delivered."

One box. On a six-month investigation. There should have been stacks and stacks of reports particularly General Progress Reports—GPRs— where detectives recorded notes. Those GPRs were what he needed. Typically handwritten by the detectives, the reports told the story of who said what. Anything on the investigation's progress should have been documented for use in trial.

So why did Zac only have one small box?

He'd have to track down the old prosecutor— the one who'd been fired by the new State's Attorney—to see what happened to the rest of the documentation. *Yeah, he'll be more than willing to talk.*

Zac stood, grabbed the box and set it on his desk. At least it had some weight to it. Inside he found a few supplementary reports, along with a lineup report. He perused one of the pages for any mention of a white shirt. Nothing. He checked the next page. Nothing.

Not off to a good start. He continued flipping through the files. Nothing about a white shirt. He dropped the stack of papers back in the box and propped his hands on his hips. He'd have to read through every document and study it.

Someone told the detectives that Brian Sinclair was wearing a white shirt that night and it wasn't their star witness. That guy had only confirmed the shirt's color. Zac considered the guy's statement, rolled it around in his mind. *Massaged* it. What he came up with was that the detectives, in a typically aggressive move, had convinced the witness they had Brian Sinclair dead to rights and all they needed was corroboration on the white shirt.

Which they got. *Hello, video.* If he couldn't discredit this sucker, Penny would argue that Sinclair's constitutional rights under *Giglio v. the United States* had been violated. In *Giglio* the Supreme Court ruled that the prosecution had to disclose all information related to the credibility of a prosecution witness, including law enforcement officials.

Bottom line, if the cops had pressured the witness into falsely identifying Brian Sinclair, his testimony could be thrown out.

And then they'd be screwed.

EMMA FOUGHT THE stampede of people exiting the building and rode the elevator to the eighth floor. As suspected, Zac was still at his desk, his big shoulders hunched over a legal pad as he took notes. A fierce longing—that black emptiness— tore at her. She'd always been drawn to men with big shoulders and the way her smaller body folded into the warmth and security of being held. *Pfft.* Right now she couldn't remember the last time she'd gone out with a man, never mind been held.

Dwelling on it wouldn't help her. She'd have to do what she always did and keep her focus on Brian. Then she'd pick up the pieces of her life.

She knocked on the open door.

"Enter," Zac said, his gaze glued to his notes.

"Hello again."

His head snapped up and a bit of his short blond hair flopped to his forehead. A sudden urge to fix the disturbed strands twitched in her fingers. Wow. Clearly she'd been without male companionship for too long. Even so, this was the man who wanted to keep her brother in prison. She had no business thinking about her hands on him.

"Ms. Sinclair?"

She stepped into the office, keeping back a couple of feet from the desk. "Hi, Zac. And it's Emma."

He dropped his pen and reclined in his squeaky chair. "Can I help you with something?"

You sure can. She waggled her phone. "I just took a call from a friend of Brian's."

The idea that she should have checked with Penny before talking to the prosecutor flashed through her mind. Maybe she'd been too hasty, but that had never stopped her before. Her brain functioned better this way, always moving and jumping from assignment to assignment. Fighting her brother's legal battle, until now, had been a solitary endeavor, and she had simply not considered that she had an ally. Next time, she'd consult with Penny. Next time.

She stepped closer to the desk and met Zac's questioning gaze. "Melody was with my brother around the time of the murder."

Zac opened his mouth and Emma held up her hand. "Let me finish. I know what Melody says doesn't prove anything, heard it a hundred times. However, she told me she turned over a receipt from the parking garage near the club."

"And?"

So smug. "I have boxes and boxes of information regarding my brother's case. Eighteen to be exact. They're stacked in my mother's basement. Three high, six across. I guess you could say I've amassed one box for every month since his conviction."

"Really," Zac said, his voice rising in a mix of wonder and maybe, just maybe, respect.

Not so smug anymore, huh? "I've never seen a receipt from a parking garage."

"With eighteen boxes, you don't think you could have missed it? And I'm sure you realize that a receipt won't prove his whereabouts."

There went the respect. Lawyers. Always vying for the mental edge.

"I do realize that. My concern is why I didn't know about this receipt and what other information I might not know about. I'd like a copy of the receipt."

He remained silent, his gaze on hers, measuring, waiting for her to cower.

"Zac, I'm happy to call Penny and make her aware of it. I'm sure *you* realize that all evidence must be shared with the defense." For kicks, she grinned at him.

He sat forward, his elbows propped on the desk, all Mr. I-won't-be-taken-down-by-a-law-student. "You and my sister will get along great."

"Excellent. I'd like the receipt, please."

"Sure." He pointed at the open box on his desk. "It's probably in here."

Slowly, she turned toward a brown banker's box sitting on the desk. The lid was off, but nowhere in sight.

One box.

A small box at that.

"Those are my brother's files?" She surveyed the office. "Where are the rest of them?"

Zac stood, his tall frame looming over the desk, his focus on the files. "We'll start with this one."

A niggling panic curled in Emma's stomach. "Tell me there's more than this. *Tell me* my brother wasn't convicted of murder based on half a box of files."

The prosecutor wouldn't look at her. Not even

a glance. He busied himself sifting through the box. Her brother's freedom rested on the contents of one minuscule box. How dare they. Eighteen months of keeping Brian from descending into emotional hell, eighteen months of her digging in, eighteen months of begging anyone who'd listen for help—it all bubbled inside. Emma locked her jaw and gutted her way through an explosion of anger that singed her. Just burned her alive from inside. These people were so callous.

She grasped the upper part of the box and yanked it toward her. Finally, he looked at her and if his eyes were a bit hard and unyielding, well, too bad. "Tell me there's more." But darn it, her voice cracked. Emma Sinclair wasn't so tough.

He continued to stare, but something flicked in his blue eyes and softened them. "Right now, this is all I have. There's more. On a six-month investigation, there has to be more."

"Where is it?"

He propped his hands on his hips and shook

his head. Emma folded her arms and waited. She wanted to know where those files were.

"Emma, I'm not about to go into court without every scrap of evidence from the first trial. A young woman is dead and I want her killer locked up, but if your brother is innocent, I'll be the first one to say so."

Brief silence filled the room. He hadn't answered her question about the whereabouts of the rest of the files. She could argue, kick up a fuss about the injustice of it all, but what was the point? All she'd do was alienate the man responsible for keeping her brother in prison. That didn't seem like a class-A plan.

Plus, for some reason, she believed him. Maybe it was his eyes and the way they snapped from hard to sparkly or the way his confidence displayed strength and a willingness to fight, but above all, Zac Hennings screamed of honor and truth.

Emma imagined that not much rattled him and she suddenly had a keen desire to see him in action, in front of a judge and jury, arguing his cases. Maybe she'd make a research trip to the courthouse and size up the enemy. She'd always believed there were multiple ways to win any brawl. Pinpointing her opponent's strengths— and weaknesses—was one of them.

Yes, a trip to the courthouse was definitely in her near future.

She shoved the box back at him. "I still want a copy of that receipt. If you don't have it, I'll have Melody call her credit card company. Either way, I'm getting that receipt."

After a long stare, one where the side of his mouth tugged into a brief smile, he dug through the box and pulled out a thick manila envelope. "I *should* advise you that I'll have everything copied and sent to Penny's office. That's what I *should* do."

"But you're not going to?"

"No. And it's highly improper. The receipt you want is probably in this envelope. I'll go through it with you. Document everything. That's the best I can do."

THERE WAS NO damn receipt. Zac sat back and watched cute, pain-in-the-butt Emma Sinclair sift through the last stack of papers from the banker's box. They'd gone through the whole box—not that there was much of it—and nothing.

What was it with this case? He'd barely started and already everything felt…off.

Emma restacked the pages she'd just gone through and shoved them back into the envelope. "No receipt."

"I'll look into it. Right now, in fact." He picked up his phone and dialed Area 2 headquarters to speak with John Cutler, one of the detectives who had investigated the case. This guy was legendary in Cook County. The cops often joked that he could squeeze a confession out of a brick. Problem was, some of those confessions got recanted. In this particular case, Brian Sinclair had never confessed. Detectives had kept him in an interview room—some would call it an interrogation room, but cops didn't like to use that term—and questioned him for more than a day, never letting him rest, never letting him eat and never hearing a confession.

Then the first of his four public defenders showed up. From what Zac remembered, one PD died—died for God's sake—one got fired, the third quit and finally, Brian Sinclair wound up with Alex Belson, an attorney Zac had faced in court many times and had no problems with. Some of the PDs were tough, never willing to stipulate to anything. Belson, though, was reasonable. Zac could call him up, talk about a case and they'd hammer out a deal to take to the judge. He never minded calls with Alex.

Zac was not a fan of Detective Cutler, however. His tactics were too rogue. Any confession pried free by Cutler always received extra scrutiny. Zac wasn't about to head into court and have the confession thrown out because the suspect's rights had been violated. No. Chance.

He waited on hold for Cutler. Emma sat across from him, her back straight and her dark eyes focused. Maybe her shoulder-length brown hair was rumpled from her fingers rifling through it, but otherwise, she was all business, and he pretty much assumed she wouldn't leave until he gave her something. And a dinner invitation probably wouldn't do it.

As a man who liked a challenge, he appreciated her ferocity. Her determination to find justice in a case that had more turns than a scenic drive. It didn't hurt that he found her easy on the eyes. Not in a flashy, made-up way, like a lot of the women he'd dated. Why he went for those women was no mystery and it was definitely nothing deep. Guys were guys and Zac supposed most enjoyed the company, among other things, of a beautiful woman.

Emma was different. She had a no-frills, natural beauty that left his chest a little tight and if she'd been anyone else, just an average woman he'd met, he'd have asked her out. Plain and simple.

Judging by the intensity of her beautiful brown eyes, she wanted to skin him.

The receptionist came back on the line and informed him that the detective was out. *Of course he was.*

"Thanks," Zac said. "Have him call me ASAP." He rattled off his work cell phone number and disconnected the call. "He's on a case," Zac told Emma.

She nodded then stood. "Obviously, Penny will need a copy of everything in this box."

She turned to leave, her body stiff and distant, and something pulled Zac out of his chair. Damned if he'd let her leave like this. Why he cared, he didn't know, but he did—massively. He hustled around the desk. "Emma, look, I don't know what's going on with the case files, but I'll figure it out. One way or another, I'll figure it out."

"Yeah, because your job is to keep my brother in prison. You want to *win*."

"If he's guilty, you bet I do. But if he's innocent, if his rights were violated and you can prove that, he'll get a new trial. That's the way our system works. Nothing I can do to change that. Nor do I want to."

She eyed him. "What do you think?"

"About?"

She waved at the files on his desk. "Looking at that box, do you think my brother's rights were violated?"

Not a chance I'm answering that one, sweetheart. "I think we're missing the rest of the files. *I* think we'll find them and then I'll get a clearer picture of this case. Until then, I believe his rights were not violated and he was convicted based on solid evidence."

She smiled. "Right. That's what you have to believe. Something tells me that, down deep—" she placed her index finger in the center of his chest and pushed "—right here, you don't necessarily agree with what you have to believe."

At her touch, heat radiated through his gut. He was no saint and willing women weren't all that hard to come by when he put some effort into it, but he could honestly say he hadn't felt that kind of fire in a long time. Whether it was wishful thinking or simply wanting action, he didn't know, but he liked it. Given his current status as the prosecutor on her brother's case, thinking like that would lead him nowhere good.

Emma snatched her finger back. He smiled and her cheeks immediately flushed. *Too damn cute.* Even if he should be running like hell.

"I need to go," she said.

For safety, Zac stepped far enough out of reach so he didn't do something stupid and touch her. "Yes, you do."

He watched her leave the office while his pulse triple-timed. A career-making case and he was having carnal thoughts about the convicted man's sister. Talk about a brilliant way to screw up.

Time to refocus and get organized. Zac dialed Alex Belson to find out where all the evidence for this case was. In a matter of one business day, Zac had fallen way behind on a case that should have been a slam dunk. A damn murder conviction and he had no files.

"Alex, hey, it's Zac Hennings."

"Hang on." Alex said something to someone on the other end then came back to him. "Sorry. Madhouse. What's up?"

"The Sinclair case. What the heck happened here? I've got one box—half full. I should have a truckload."

Alex groaned. "I feel for ya, man. I inherited exactly what you got."

"And?"

"And what? I was the fourth PD to handle this guy. I backtracked, though. The first guy died— as in keeled over out of the blue. And the other two guys aren't with the PD's Office anymore. I'm guessing when the first guy crapped out, some of his files were never recovered. Then the other two guys left and all I could salvage was what was in that box."

A murder case with no evidence. Zac dug his fingertips into his forehead. He'd have to track down the two remaining PDs, wherever they might be. If he had a knife, he'd gut himself. "You're telling me that one box is all there is?"

"As far as I know. I don't have investigators just sitting around here. Plus, we're dealing with a cop's daughter as the victim. Dude, I knew going in I was going to lose. The blue wall wasn't coming down on this one."

Cops in Chicago were legendary for their ability to keep quiet about crimes involving other cops. Chicago's blue wall wasn't cement—that sucker was solid steel—and the detectives didn't bend over to help the defense. For the most part, Chicago detectives were honest investigators who worked until they reached logical conclusions. In some cases, hunches, whether right or wrong, guided them, made them feel someone's guilt deep in their bones. Magicians that they were, they found a way to organize the evidence so it helped get a conviction.

In the case of Chelsea Moore, detectives chipped away until the evidence fit. They would have made it fit for Dave. In a way, Zac understood.

And that scared the hell out of him.

"I'll tell you one thing, though," Alex said. "Emma Sinclair made for a great investigator. She hammered me about the victim's boyfriend. Ex-boyfriend. Ben Leeks Jr."

Zac wrote down the name. "What about him?"

"His father—Ben Leeks—is an Area 1 detective."

Zac's stomach pitched. He shot a glance at the box of evidence. There had to be something in there about the boyfriend. "Was he questioned?"

"According to the detectives, he was cleared early on. The PD before me talked to the kid. Nothing there."

"I'm guessing Emma wasn't happy."

"She thought it was too convenient. Can't say I blamed her. I went with what I had."

After three other PDs had already gone with it. Total snake pit. Zac made another note to look into the boyfriend. "What happened with the boy-friend?"

"Chelsea's friend said the kid was abusive. Smacked her around some."

"And he was *cleared?*"

"The blue wall, my friend, the blue wall."

Zac wrote *blue wall* on his notepad and then slashed a giant X through it. If it took a blow torch, he'd burn through that steel wall.

Chapter Three

After blowing off class on Friday morning and visiting Brian, Emma flew down the expressway toward home. Lately it seemed she was always in a hurry to get somewhere while never really reaching the place she wanted to be. Today however, her optimism had hit a two-year high. During their visit, Brian had made adjustments to her time line. How those adjustments would differ from the video and trial transcripts, she wasn't sure, but she'd find out soon enough by comparing them.

Emma sang along with the radio. She felt as if things were looking up. Even if the gray sky, in complete contrast to her mood, hung dull and lifeless, it wouldn't dampen her sunny mood. Brian had stayed subdued about their new lawyer. *Defense mechanism.* Her younger brother lived in a six-by-six cell. Hope ran thin for him.

Emma's cell phone rang and she punched the Bluetooth.

"Helloooo?" she sang.

"Penny Hennings here. Where are you?"

Hello to you, too, Penny. Then again, Emma didn't need her pro bono lawyer to be her friend. She needed her to give Brian his life back.

"I'm coming from seeing Brian. Thirty minutes from downtown. Why?"

"I'm heading to court. I need my intern's help. Can you get to the parking garage next to Magic?"

Emma stuck out her bottom lip. "The nightclub?"

"The one and only. I had one of our investigators call the garage owner about the missing receipt. He has an office across the street from the garage above the sub shop. He also has five years of security backups and can pull the date we need. I love technology."

Now this could be good. "He's willing to let me look through them?"

"Yes. And if you find anything, he'll give us a copy. I'll call Zac. I want someone from the State's Attorney's Office to be with you so they can't accuse us of tampering. The chain of custody on this will be rock solid. Ha! My brother will have a cow. I cannot wait. Seriously, I love my job sometimes."

Maybe Zac was right about his sister being nuts. Sanity issues aside, this might be another lead. "I'll take care of it."

Emma arrived at the garage, parked and made her way across the street. A lunch rush descended on the sub shop and, with her metabolism reminding her that she'd only had a banana for breakfast, she contemplated grabbing a sandwich on the way out. Next to the sub shop was a door marked ENGLAND MANAGEMENT. She swung through the door and walked up the stairwell.

At the top of the stairs she found a second glass door. The receptionist glanced up and waved Emma in.

"Hi. I'm Emma Sinclair."

The receptionist smiled. "He's expecting you. Come in."

Emma was ushered down the short, carpeted hallway to an office where a man sat at a metal-framed desk. The receptionist waved her in and the man stood up. He wore khaki pants and a long-sleeved golf shirt that stretched across his protruding belly. She guessed his age at about fifty, but she never was any good at figuring out a person's age. His lips curved into a welcoming grin and the wrinkles around his eyes bunched. Nice smile. Emma returned the gesture. She'd come to appreciate someone smiling at the sister of a man convicted of murder. Even if that man were innocent, most people didn't take the time to think of her feelings in that regard.

"I'm Emma Sinclair. I believe Penny Hennings told you to expect me."

"Sure thing. I'm Glen. Glen Beckett. Have a seat." He waved her over to one of the two chairs in front of the desk. "You know the date you're looking for?"

I sure do. "Yes. March 21st—two years ago. Not last March."

Glen swung to the computer and grabbed the mouse. Emma leaned forward. "On second thought, Glen, would you please wait one second? Someone is meeting me here and I don't want to start without him. Let me make a quick call."

She dialed Penny, who picked up on the second ring. "He's coming."

"Who?"

"Zac."

"Really? Not an investigator?"

"Zac's court appearance was continued and my brother is no fool. If I'm requesting someone be with you, he knows I'm not playing games. My extremely smart brother wants to see for himself what evidence I'm going to hit him with."

The door behind Emma flew open and Zac

Hennings, all wide shoulders and six-foot-plus of him, marched into the office. For reasons she didn't understand herself, Emma stepped back. Zac certainly knew how to enter a room and command it.

"He's here." Emma disconnected and shoved the phone in her jacket pocket. "Hi."

Zac nodded. "Emma." He turned to Glen, held his hand out. "Zac Hennings. I'm an Assistant Cook County State's Attorney."

"Holy..." Glen shot a look at Emma then went back to Zac.

"I'm only here to authenticate the video *if* we find something."

"Oh," Emma said. "We'll find something. My brother said he walked Melody to her car and she drove him back to Magic."

Glen faced his computer again. "Then we should have it. The camera by the exit records all vehicles as they leave. Do you know what time?"

"Somewhere around 12:30 a.m."

A few clicks later a video popped onto the

screen. Emma jumped out of her seat and crashed into Zac, her shoulder nailing him right in the solar plexus as they both attempted to round the desk. He let out a whoosh of air and clasped both her arms to keep her from stumbling. Emma stared down at his hands—good strong hands that had to be capable of all sorts of things—and sucked in a breath.

"Sorry!" she said. "So sorry. Are you okay?"

"I'm fine." He waved her through. "Go ahead. You'll recognize him before I will."

She wedged herself between Zac and the desk and stood next to Glen, who scrolled through a video while checking the time stamp.

"I can stop it around 12:25, if you want. Then you can watch it in slow motion."

"Thank you," Emma said.

Behind her, Zac inched up, his body not touching hers, but close enough that an awareness made it hard to focus. He had that way about him. Commanding, but reserved. Somehow she didn't think Zac Hennings had to beat on his chest and holler in order to control a room. He had a sense of authority about him that completely unnerved her.

She kind of liked that. Or maybe she was just lonely. Either way, she couldn't think too much about it. Her loneliness depressed her and she had no interest in analyzing that fact. Or the fact that he was the prosecutor on her brother's case. What a mess that would be. Allowing herself to want him darn near guaranteed another heartbreak.

"Do we know what kind of car we're looking for?" Glen asked.

Emma stepped forward, adding space between her and hunky Zac Hennings. "It's a Dodge Neon."

Zac nodded and three pairs of eyes focused on the screen. Three minutes later, Emma checked the time stamp again. 12:35. No Dodge Neon. No Melody. No Brian.

Come on. Inside her shoe, she wiggled her toes. Her head pounded as the seconds ticked away. *Please be there*.

"There it is!" Glen yelled.

Emma brought her gaze to the car on the screen. The pounding in her head tripled and she squeezed her fingers into fists. *This could be it.*

Zac leaned closer, his chest nudging Emma's shoulder. "Can you slow this down?"

Had they been anywhere else, she would have poked him with her elbow and given him the back-off-buddy look, but she refused to take her eyes off that screen.

Glen tapped at the mouse and the car slowed to barely moving as it proceeded through the open gate.

"Here we go. This should be it," Emma said as two figures—one male and one female—came into view. As the car rolled forward, the camera finally captured their faces and—bang—there was her brother's smiling face. Energy roared into her, made her a little lightheaded, and moisture filled her mouth. She swallowed once, twice. *He's there.*

"Freeze it," she yelled before the car drove off

screen. She turned to Zac. "That's him. That's Brian. And Melody."

"12:37," he said. "Okay."

"Okay? Okay what?"

Zac shrugged. "We have him on tape. This gets admitted into evidence." He turned to Glen. "I'll need a copy of this video."

Clearly, the prosecutor didn't want to say another thing in front of Glen. Fine. She'd wait. At least until they got outside. Then they'd chat.

"Make it two," Emma said.

ZAC STEPPED ONTO the sidewalk and contemplated jumping in front of the bus pulling up to the curb. His sister would go crazy over this video. Not only would she smell the blood, she'd swim faster to get to it.

Emma had stayed on his heels on the way down to the building exit and parked herself in front of him. Forget the impending self-inflicted death.

"12:37," she said. "That proves where he was."

"Yes. At 12:37. Doesn't necessarily help, though.

We have the time of the murder narrowed to an hour. He could have done it *after* Melody dropped him back at the club."

She flapped her arms. "Oh, please. This is a guy who worried enough about his friend to walk her back to her car and then ride out of the garage with her. You think he goes from there to killing someone? It makes no sense."

The bus pulled away with a whoosh and left a batch of engine fumes to poison Zac's lungs. Once again he contemplated the bus. *Should have jumped.* He looked back at Emma. "Nothing ever makes sense in my job. I go with the evidence. Tell me about the victim's ex-boyfriend and the abuse."

Emma jerked her head back and stared up at him with those big brown eyes that made him think of liquid chocolate and all the things he liked to do with it. Now he'd have to figure out a way to get *that* thought out of his mind.

"Yeah," he said. "I know about that. I talked to your brother's public defender. He said you hammered him about the ex-boyfriend. So tell me because there's nothing in that box of files about it and that doesn't sit right with me."

Emma hesitated, twisting her lips for a second and—yeah—he'd have to get those lips, along with the liquid chocolate, out of his head, too.

"I was upset that the police weren't talking about the boyfriend. Brian knew Chelsea Moore casually. They were the same age and were regulars at Magic. Brian told me she'd texted him a few times after she'd broken up with her boyfriend. I don't think Brian was interested in her in a—well—sexual way so he didn't pursue her. When he was questioned, he asked the police about her ex-boyfriend. They did nothing with it."

"How do you know?"

"I asked the public defender. The guy before Alex Belson. He didn't have anything on it."

"Then how do you know the ex was abusive?"

"Well, Zac," Emma said, layering on the sarcasm. "I did something that was pure investigative genius. I did something the Chicago P.D. never thought of doing."

Here we go. "Ditch the drama, Emma. I get it."

She held up a finger. "I talked to the victim's friends. Miraculous, isn't it?"

Zac rolled his eyes, but he couldn't blame her for the attitude. If it had been one of his siblings on trial, he'd feel that same burning, festering anger. This whole thing stunk of cops trying to protect the ex-boyfriend, who also happened to be the son of a cop.

The blue wall.

He grabbed Emma's elbow and ushered her to the corner. "Are you parked in the garage?"

"Yes. I need a sandwich first. I haven't eaten all day."

"Fine. I'll wait for you and then walk you to your car. Then I have a couple of detectives to talk to."

DETECTIVE JOHN CUTLER marched into Zac's office wearing a wrinkled blue sport coat and a scowl. The man didn't like being summoned to an ASA's office in the middle of the day. Zac didn't care.

Not when one of Cutler's investigations was about to be sliced and diced in court and Zac would be the one taking the hit.

He tossed a pen on his stacked desk and leaned back in his chair. "Have a seat, detective."

Cutler stared down at the two chairs, curled his lip at the one with the stack of file folders and dropped his bloated body into the vacant one. He spent a few seconds shifting into what would have to pass as a comfortable position, then stretched his neck where loose skin spilled over his collar.

Zac waited. Why not? No sense giving the detective the ever-important mental edge. Nope. Zac would control the festivities.

Finally, Cutler held up his hands. "What do you need?"

Zac leaned over, scooped a box off the floor and set it on the desk. "The Sinclair case. These are the files. On a *six-month* investigation. Am I missing something?"

Cutler's gaze tracked left then came back to Zac. "How do I know what your office did with the files?"

Not an answer. "Is this box everything? If you tell me *yes,* then I work with what I have. If you tell me no, we have missing evidence."

Cutler folded his hands across his belly and tapped his index fingers. "I'd have to look through the box. See what's there."

"Sure." Cutler got up to leave. "I'm not finished, detective."

The man made a show of checking his watch, and Zac nearly laughed. He'd grown up in a household that produced three lawyers. He thrived on conflict.

Cutler reclaimed his seat.

"Couple of things," Zac said. "What do you remember about a parking garage receipt given to you by Melody—" he checked his legal pad "—Clayton? She's a friend of Brian Sinclair who claims he was with her around the time of the murder."

Slowly, Cutler shook his head.

Patience, Zac. Patience. "You don't remember a receipt?"

"No. She could have given it to Steve and I wasn't aware."

"Steve Bennett? The other detective?"

"Yes."

Sure, another dead guy to blame. This case was rife with dead guys. "I'll look into that. I'm assuming you viewed the video I sent over. What do you remember about the witness?"

Cutler shrugged. "It's not like we coerced him. We showed him a six-pack, helped him narrow it down."

Helped him narrow it down… "And what about the white shirt? Who told him Brian Sinclair was wearing a white shirt?"

"I don't know anything about that. That must have been Steve."

Of course.

Zac jotted more notes and the detective tugged on his too-tight collar again. *Yes, detective, you should be nervous.* The truth was, Zac scribbled gibberish. The Area 2 detectives weren't the only ones who knew how to play mind games.

"The victim's friend told Emma Sinclair that Ben Leeks—I'm sure you're aware he's the son of a Chicago P.D. detective—was abusive."

Cutler shot Zac a hard look. Well, maybe *Cutler* thought it was a hard look. Zac thought it was more of a desperate, defensive man's way of trying to intimidate an opponent. "The kid was cleared early on."

"Cleared how?"

"He was inside the club. We had witnesses who saw him getting busy with some brunette. He didn't leave the club until closing. When he did leave, he left with a group and they all went to the diner down the street."

Zac nodded. "I need names. They're not in the case file."

Cutler grabbed one of the armrests and shifted

his big body. "I told you I don't have anything. I turned over all the reports."

"Even the GPRs?" Zac smacked his knuckle against the box. "I didn't see any GPRs."

"I turned over *everything.*"

"Did you write up any GPRs?"

Again the detective tried a hard look and Zac angled forward. "I'm aware that you're not happy being questioned. I don't care. I'm about to get hauled into court to defend your work. My guess is you want me to feel confident about that work. I'm far from confident. Cut the nonsense and answer my questions."

Cutler sighed. "I wrote up GPRs. I don't know what happened to them."

"Did you make copies?"

"No."

"Of course you didn't. Does it shock you that reports pertaining to the allegedly abusive son of a detective were not submitted into evidence for a murder trial?"

Cutler stayed silent. The blue wall.

Zac eased his chair up to the desk and put the box back on the floor. "I think we're done. For now."

The detective sat across from him, his breaths coming in short, heavy bursts and his cheeks flamed. He was obviously steaming mad.

Good.

Zac was about to get his butt handed to him—by his baby sister, no less—and he wasn't going down alone. Ignoring the about-to-be-raging bull across from him, he flipped open one of the many file folders on his desk and began reading. Cutler finally pushed himself out of his chair.

"That Sinclair kid is guilty," he said. "No two ways about it."

Zac didn't bother to look up. "A video of him leaving the parking garage at 12:37 might say otherwise. Buckle up, detective. We're about to go for a rough ride."

EMMA PULLED INTO the driveway at 12:15 that night after enduring Friday-night chaos at the restaurant. As usual, Mom had left the porch and overhead garage lights on. Even now, with a son in prison, Mom worried about her children being out late.

It never ends for her.

Emma gathered her apron and shoved the car door open. Her feet hit the pavement and she nearly groaned. Hauling trays all night had left her arms and back aching and, combined with her beat-up feet, she longed for her bed.

Nothing about waitressing was easy, but the money was good. Better than good since she'd gotten lucky and landed a job in an upscale steak place. Still, she craved the day when she'd go back to an office job, sit behind a desk and leave the body aches behind.

Soon, Emma. If her plan worked and Brian came home, she'd have her life and a chance at a normal schedule back. She could attend law school at night, allowing her to take a nine-to-five job. Heck, maybe Penny would hire her as an assistant.

Emma hip-checked her car door shut and hit the LOCK button. A loud beep-beep sounded. Out of habit, she glanced behind her. Nothing there. Their neighborhood had always been safe, but she'd learned to be cautious wherever she went. Criminals didn't necessarily care what neighborhood they were in if the target appeared easy.

Humming to herself for a distraction until she reached the front door, she tossed her apron over her shoulder. She'd throw it and her uniform in the washer before bed so she'd have it for tomorrow.

"Ms. Sinclair?"

Emma froze, her body literally halting in place, unable to move. Deep—*male*—voice behind her. *He knows my name.* An onslaught of blood shot to her temples. Car key pointed out, she spun around. A man wearing an unzipped brown leather jacket, dark shirt—no buttons—and jeans stood in the tiny driveway directly under the garage light. He wasn't tall, but he appeared fit. Muscular. Tough.

Get a description.

Short, darkish hair that was almost black. No gray. She guessed he was in his late forties. His nose was wide and crooked, broken a few times maybe.

He stepped toward her. *Don't let him get too close.* She backed away, key still in hand, ready to poke an eye, if necessary. He grinned. A disgusting I've-got-you grin that pinched Emma's throat. She swallowed once, gripped the key harder.

"Ms. Sinclair, relax. I'm Detective Ben Leeks, Chicago P.D."

Emma let out a long breath, but paralyzing tension racked her shoulders. No straight-up detective would be visiting her house at this hour, particularly the father of a guy whose girlfriend had been murdered. With her free hand, she reached into her jacket pocket for her phone. Worst case, she'd hold the panic button on her key ring to trigger the car's horn and then dial 9-1-1.

"Detective, it's late. This is inappropriate."

Slowly, she backed toward the porch. A car drove by. *Scream.* That's what she should do.

Except she might wind up looking like a lunatic and lunatics never got their brother's convictions overturned.

The detective didn't move. Simply stood there, arms loose at his sides, posture erect, but casual, completely nonthreatening. "No judge in Cook County will overturn *that* conviction. Get comfortable with your brother in prison and stop making trouble. Troublemakers in this city get dealt with. Sometimes the hard way."

Emma stood in a sort of detached shock. Tremors erupted over her body, that nasty prickling, digging into her limbs and making her itch. He strolled out of the driveway, just a man enjoying an early spring night. *Get in the house.* She ran toward the door, shoved the key at the lock with trembling hands and missed. She glanced over her shoulder again, saw no one and breathed in. *Get inside.* On the second try, the key connected and she stormed into the house, throwing the dead bolt then falling against the door.

He'd just threatened her.

Maybe it wasn't an overt threat. Without a doubt he'd deny it if she flung an accusation his way, but they both knew he'd just delivered a message.

All that was left now was to decide what she'd do about that message.

Chapter Four

One thing Zac didn't expect to hear at seven o'clock on a Saturday morning was his crazy sister pounding on his door. The sound drove through his skull like a pickax. What the heck was she doing? Couldn't a guy get a break and sleep in on his day off? He should never have given her a key to the first-floor entry. And for that matter, why didn't she use her *other* key to open the inside door?

He rolled out of bed, blinked a few times against the shaft of sunlight seeping through the blinds and grabbed a pair of track pants from the chair. Too damn early for this. The way she was carrying on she'd wake up the other two tenants in the house. Worse, he was on the second floor, so the two remaining apartments would have equal opportunity to hear the racket. After jamming his legs into his pants, he grabbed last night's T-shirt from the floor and decided it would do. Temporarily.

"Zachary! Open this door."

"Keep your skirt on, Pen. I'm coming. Why didn't you use your key?"

Prepared to broil her, he ripped open the door and there she stood in a blinding bright pink coat. He closed his eyes, drove his fingers into them. "You look like a popsicle. Seriously, you need to tone that down."

When he opened his eyes again, his gaze shot to movement behind the popsicle. Instantly his face got hot. A sizzling burn straight to his cheeks because his crazy sister had brought Emma Sinclair—in a knit cap and white trench coat that made him think about stripping them off her—to visit.

Pen pushed by him, stomped into his apartment

and jerked her thumb behind her. "She's why I didn't use my key. How did I know if you'd be naked in here? Or if you had company."

Emma remained standing in the hallway and he waved her in. "You might as well come in. Excuse the mess. And that I'm not appropriately dressed for a business meeting." He turned to his sister. "In my *apartment*. On my day *off*."

"Blah, blah, blah," Penny said. "You won't believe this one, Zachary."

"I'm sure you'll enlighten me."

"Bet your butt, I will. Detective Ben Leeks visited Emma last night at her house. He was waiting for her, *stalking* her, when she came home from work at one o'clock in the morning."

Zac shifted his gaze to Emma who stood quietly in the middle of his living room, staring at him and his bed head. He might be a little slow on the uptake this morning but last he'd checked, his hearing was pretty good and he thought his nutty sister had just told him Emma had received a visit from a potential suspect's cop father.

"He did *what?*"

The thing he did not need in this already puzzling case was some amped-up detective with a direct link to the proceedings screwing around.

Penny, ever the drama queen, threw her hands up. "Marched right up her driveway and scared the daylights out of her."

Zac went back to Emma, studied her face for any sign of trauma. Nothing there. Only soft lips and those lustful wide eyes. "Are you okay?"

Pen's phone rang. The theme from *The Godfather.* "Ooh," she said. "This is Dad. Hang on." She retrieved the phone from the suitcase-slash-purse she carried. "Hi, Dad."

He faced Emma. "She gave my father *The Godfather* theme as a ringtone. I told you she was whacked."

Penny's eyebrows hitched up. "Sure. Got it. I'm on it, Dad." She disconnected. "I have to go."

"*What?*" Zac said for what felt like the tenth time. "You drop this on me and you're leaving?"

He gestured to his clothing, then to Emma.

"I have to go. The son of one of our clients got arrested. Mom and Dad left for Wisconsin early and they're already at the lake house. He needs me to get the guy out of lockup and I'm not telling our father no." She turned to Emma. "I'm sorry to do this to you. Can you fill Zac in and then grab a cab home?"

Emma slid her gaze to Zac, hesitated, then went back to Penny. "Um, sure."

In a blur of pink, Penny strode to the door and Zac pulled it open for her. Leave it to her to install Emma and her gorgeous brown eyes in his apartment and then bolt. Bad enough that his thoughts had been dropping to the gutter ever since Emma had put her hand on his chest a day-and-a-half ago, now he had to be alone with her in his apartment. Did he mention alone? *Damn Penny.* "I'll take her home. Why should she take a cab?"

His sister patted his cheek. "Good boy, Zachary. Don't forget, we have to be at the lake by five today. Don't be late. Mom will kill you. And me because you're my driver."

"I won't be late."

He shut the door and faced Emma, the woman he was terrified to be alone with in his apartment. Only slightly awkward, this situation. "Sorry about waking you up," she said. "I made the mistake of telling your sister I had the morning and early afternoon open. Apparently she thinks that means it's okay to call me at 6:00 a.m."

Zac laughed. "I swear she's a vampire. She's always been this way. She can function on five hours' sleep and I need a ton. How is that fair when we come from the same gene pool?"

"I don't know. Don't get me wrong, I'm not complaining. I appreciate her dedication."

"She's dedicated all right. I love that about her. Just not on a Saturday. When I'm sleeping."

Emma glanced around the apartment. Her stare landed on the kitchen doorway at the end of the hall. Excellent idea. Safest room. He could throw a pot of coffee together. The caffeine would jump-start him and give him something to do with his hands. Considering his hands wouldn't mind stripping that coat off Emma Sinclair. "How about coffee?"

She nodded and followed him into the kitchen where his table sat buried under case files, reminding him that he should get a damn life and invite people over once in a while.

"I guess you don't eat in the kitchen much?"

"There's one spot cleared. I usually sit there and read while I'm eating." He cleared a second spot. At least now they could both sit.

"So, the files in your office and all of these—" she pointed "—are all your cases?"

"Yeah. No time to be bored."

He scooped coffee into the basket, filled the reservoir and hit the button. "Tell me about the detective."

"Creep. He was waiting for me when I got home last night. I didn't see him when I pulled in, but by the time I got near the front door, he was in the driveway."

Zac leaned against the counter and folded his arms. "What time was this?"

"About twelve-fifteen."

Of all the idiot things. Sure he was some hot-shot detective everyone in the P.D. either feared or worshipped, but if the guy thought Zac would let him interfere with his case, Ben Leeks had another think coming.

Zac nodded. "Putting aside the fact that it's not all that safe for you to be driving around by yourself so late—"

A flush of red fired Emma's cheeks and she snapped her head up. "*Excuse* me? Some rogue detective pays me a visit in the middle of the night and it's *my* fault?"

"I didn't say that. And you didn't let me finish."

But—wow—the woman was steamed in a big way. He'd better fix this quick. He held his hands up. "I'm sorry. None of my business. What he did was out of line without question. I'll deal with him."

"That's more like it, Mr. Prosecutor."

Now he was Mr. Prosecutor. Perfect. Maybe he deserved that blast of frigidness. Pointing out the obvious—that a woman should not be out alone late at night—was apparently unacceptable. With the cases he'd seen—maimed women, dead women, women who'd been violated in unspeakable ways—suddenly he shouldn't warn someone the world could be an ugly place?

Or maybe his already jaded view of the world got knocked further into submission by such atrocities. Someone like Emma Sinclair, with her can-do, won't-be-beaten attitude, didn't see the world the way he did. She saw a problem and tried to fix it. Zac saw a problem and wanted to know who he could lock up.

The coffeemaker gurgled. Finally. He spun to the cabinet, pulled out two giant mugs and poured. The potent aroma of the strong brew drifted toward him and something in his brain popped. "Milk or sugar?"

"Black with sugar."

From the same cabinet he grabbed a few packs of sweetener and handed the steaming mug over. "Tell me what Detective Leeks said."

She dug into her coat pocket and pulled out a folded piece of lined paper. "I wrote it down."

She wrote it down. Emma Sinclair would be an A-list lawyer. Before reading, he took a hit of coffee, one good gulp that burned his throat. He set the mug down, unfolded the paper and read.

Get comfortable with your brother spending his life in prison and stop making trouble. Troublemakers in this city get dealt with. Sometimes the hard way.

His neck went tight. Bam. Solid ache. He cracked it and let some of the tension snap free. In an effort not to miss anything, he went over the note a second time.

After a third read, he glanced up at Emma who had her luscious eyes focused on him. "This is exactly what he said?"

"Yes. I wrote it down the minute I got into the house. He also said no judge in Cook County would overturn Brian's conviction. I didn't write that down, though. It was too much to remember and I wanted to document the part about trouble-makers before I forgot."

Zac took another two swallows of coffee and dumped the rest in the sink. He needed to nix this quick. "Wait here. I'm grabbing a quick shower then I'll pay a visit to the good detective. You good with that?"

"Am I going with you?"

"If you want to. Otherwise, I'll take you home. This is the kind of garbage—this pressuring witnesses—that got us into this mess in the first place. He needs to be called out."

A smile crept across Emma's face. Obviously she had developed an affinity for conflict, for the clashing of wills. For *war*. Zac understood the intoxicating pull. No matter how gruesome the case, he experienced a natural high every time he stepped into a courtroom.

"I'll wait for you," Emma said.

ZAC HENNINGS MIGHT be as crazy as his sister.

Emma loved it. Every inch of it. The look on

his face when he read the note, all rock-hard and vicious, showed Emma a side of him she hadn't seen before. He may have been the enemy, but he wanted to win fair and square. She appreciated that in him. Or maybe she was looking for something to like beyond how good his butt looked in track pants.

She seriously had to get her head in the game. This guy could keep Brian in prison and pulverize what was left of her family. Thinking about him in a physical way, no matter how deprived of male attention she might be, would only destroy her.

Focus was what she needed now. She'd been fighting for justice and now she had a chance. An attraction to Zac Hennings couldn't derail that.

Not today.

Not tomorrow.

Not any day.

She took another swig of coffee. Sludge, really. Who could drink coffee so unbelievably strong?

Splayed in front of her were stacks of folders

and for no other reason than idle curiosity, not to mention boredom, she itched to take a peek.

Not happening, though. He'd left her here, trusting her not to invade his privacy. She wouldn't betray that trust. She glanced around the room. Just feet away stood the refrigerator, a plain white one with French doors and an ancient stove that anchored the laminate countertop. A no-fuss kitchen for a bachelor. Somehow she'd expected fancier from a guy whose father was a big-shot attorney. That'd teach her for prejudging.

Needing a distraction, she went to the sink, poured the sludge down the drain and heard the shower go off. Talk about idle curiosity. She wouldn't mind taking a gander at the country-club-rugged prosecutor wrapped in a towel. No shirt, skin still slick. She grunted. The way he filled out his shirts, she was darn sure it would be a pleasant experience. Yep. That would be a sight.

"Wow, Emma," she muttered. "You are a mess."

Mess or no mess, she stole a glance down the

hall to see if he'd come out of the bathroom in a towel. Nothing. Not even a glimpse.

Rotten luck. As usual.

So I'm desperate. Big deal. Between the files and Zac naked, she had to move. The living room might be a better spot. On her way down the hall, she slowed when she reached a room with a half-open door. Bedroom. For kicks, she snuck a glance. Hey, if she couldn't see him in a towel, she'd check out his bedroom. The room was surprisingly uncluttered, considering what his office and kitchen looked like. Maybe he'd thrown a pair of jeans into a corner, but the heavy cherry dresser was neat and polished.

Behind her, the bathroom door flew open and even if her mind and body brawled over whether or not to sneak a peek, she scooted away. "I'm moving to the living room," she called over her shoulder.

"Everything okay?"

Risking the sight of him in a towel, she spun around and found him fully clothed in jeans and a crisp button-down shirt. "Yep. Your files were distracting me."

He angled back to the kitchen, the potential error of his ways hitting home and she held up her hand. "I swear I didn't look. I removed my overly curious self from the area."

For many reasons.

"Thank you for not looking. None of them are your brother's files, but…"

"I know," Emma said. "As much as my brain likes activity, you trusted me. I wanted to respect that."

Zac moved closer and the smell of his soap, something clean and pure—*salt air*—reached her. His blond hair was still damp and somehow, even more than if she'd seen him in that towel, Zac Hennings drew every ounce of her attention.

"You are something else, Emma. Straightforward. No drama. I like that."

The compliment burrowed inside and a rush of happiness lit into her. *He's not the guy for you.* Even if she had thousands of arguments, none of them could be justified. Not if Brian's freedom became the casualty. She shrugged. "I am what I am. Life hasn't exactly gone as planned, but I refuse to give in to it. There's a happy ending for my family somewhere. I'm not sure when or how, but I know it's out there."

He watched her for a few seconds, his eyes intense and unwavering and all that determined male attention made her legs a little wobbly. She needed a man. Preferably one like Zac Hennings.

Soon.

Finally, he broke away. "I hope you find that happy ending. Your mother and brother are lucky to have you."

Down deep, she knew that. Sure, there were times she admitted to herself, she'd like to run away, just disappear somewhere, hit the RESET button and start over, but she didn't have it in her to walk away. She loved her family too much.

But suddenly, the small space of silence between her and Zac filled with crackling energy and Emma's pulse jackhammered. She couldn't take it anymore. All this thinking about naked, hot prosecutors and running away and freedom, it was almost too much. A prize dangling just out of reach.

"I...um." She shook her head. *Don't know.*

Zac looked away. *Thank you.* He turned to the small side table and scooped up a set of keys. "Let's hunt down our rogue detective."

Chapter Five

After calling and confirming Detective Leeks was working, Zac left Emma in the car and climbed the few stairs leading to Area 2 headquarters. The short walk gave him a minute to clear his traitorous mind because, seriously, how many times would he have to shut down thoughts of Emma under him and moaning. He had no business wanting that. Not when a botched murder investigation was involved.

Once inside the building, he identified himself and told—no asking—the desk sergeant he wanted to see Detective Leeks.

Five minutes later, he was directed down a long hallway and told to take the last doorway on the left. That last doorway, not surprisingly, was an *interview* room. These dopes thought they'd play him by letting him stew in an interrogation room. This stunt only added fuel to his already raging fire.

He yanked out a chair, settled into it, threw his shoulders back and took a breath. *He* would control this conversation. Not Leeks.

Ten minutes they made him wait. With each ticking second, Zac got more steamed, all that negative energy spewing in his mind. Contain it. That's what he'd do. Contain it and channel it. He'd been raised by a master strategist. He'd carve Leeks to pieces before he let this chump play mind games with him.

Finally, Leeks stepped into the room. The guy was a good four inches shorter than Zac, so Zac made sure to stand and greet him. Let the shorter man get a feel for looking up at him.

Leeks stared at him with dark, vacant eyes. Nothing there. No life. No anger. Nothing. After a brief stare-down, he must have come to the realization that intimidation tactics were useless. *No dice, pal.*

Leeks pursed his lips and made a smacking sound before dragging out the chair opposite Zac's.

Zac waited for him to sit, hesitated a few extra seconds, then reclaimed his chair. The detective smirked. Yeah, he knew the alpha war game of standing over someone as long as possible. At least they understood each other.

Leeks pushed up the sleeves on his sweater. Most detectives wore sport coats and dress slacks. Maybe during the week Leeks did, too. Today he wore jeans and an expensive-looking sweater.

Zac sat forward. "I'll make this quick, detective. I'm the prosecutor handling the Sinclair case. My guess is you know that already."

"Affirmative."

"Good. Let me also inform you that you are to stay away from anyone involved in this case. *Anyone.* Do you understand?"

Leeks shrugged.

"I'll take that as a yes because the next time you threaten Emma Sinclair, I'll dig up enough dirt on you that your superiors will have no choice but to relieve you of your badge."

Leeks finally sat forward, all tough-guy shrugs and grimaces. "Listen, Ivy League, I didn't threaten Emma Sinclair."

Excellent. Precisely what Zac wanted to hear. He slapped Emma's note on the table. "You didn't say this?"

Leeks eyeballed him then picked up the paper. After reading it, he tossed it back and it floated in midair for a moment, crackling in the silence.

Leaning in, Zac mirrored the detective's body language. "You expect me to believe Emma Sinclair lied when she said you walked up to her home in the middle of the night and told her troublemakers in this city get dealt with. You didn't say that?"

"Hey, Ivy League—"

"Hey, *detective,* I'm not interested in having a

conversation. I'm *telling* you what you need to do. Am I clear?"

Leeks slouched back—almost retreating, but then defiantly folding his arms across his chest. The guy's body language was all over the place.

"Yeah. You're clear. Crystal. But you better find a way to keep this guy in lockup. He murdered a young woman and his cute, defenseless sister is getting this city all churned up. Do your job, counselor."

As if he'd let this scumbag lecture him. "After the garbage you've pulled, you think I'll let you sit there and tell me how to do my job? Screw off, detective. Last I checked, my conviction rate was rock-solid. As long as I don't have overanxious cops mucking it up, we'll have a murderer behind bars." Zac stood and headed for the door. "By the way, I went to Loyola. And make sure your son is available to me."

Leeks shot out of his chair, sending the legs scraping across the cheap linoleum. "*What?*"

That extra four inches Zac had on Leeks played

nicely here. It was tough to get large with someone taller and carrying an extra thirty pounds.

"You heard me. Have your son call me. I have
questions about his relationship with Chelsea
Moore. The sooner those questions are answered,
the sooner this case goes away. I'm extending you
a courtesy here. If you and your son choose not
to take advantage of that courtesy, I'll subpoena
him. Your choice, detective, but either way, your
son will talk to me."

EMMA SAT IN ZAC'S sleek BMW, one just like
Penny's—and how cute was that?—thinking he
should be coming back any second. As curious
as she was about his meeting, boredom had set in
more than ten minutes ago. How long did it take
to go in there, tell this loser detective to back off
and come back?

Her cell phone rang. *Thank you.* Penny. "Hi."

"Hi. How'd it go with Zac?"

"Not sure yet. He's in talking with the detective now."

"OMG," Penny squealed. "I love my brother. He's so darn predictable. He's probably tearing that guy apart as we speak. Listen, Emma. Good trial lawyers know their opponent's weaknesses and use them. It doesn't hurt that our opponent happens to be my brother and he has a streak of honor in him a mile long."

"You manipulated him?"

"So harsh! I utilized my knowledge of his personality. Guaranteed he'll come out of that meeting and say he's subpoenaing Leeks's kid."

"Well, we should know shortly. I'm waiting in the car. I think it's cute that you two have the same car."

"His is two years older than mine. Our parents gave each of us one when we graduated from law school. Our older brother totaled his a year in. Those cars are the only ones they bought us. We had to pay for our first cars on our own. It was a good lesson in managing money."

Emma glanced up and spotted Zac jogging down the few steps in front of police headquarters, his long legs moving fast. "Here comes Zac. Want to hang on until he gets here?"

"You bet."

He swung into the car and Emma put the call on speaker. "I have Penny on the phone."

"Hey," he said. "Did you spring your guy?"

"I did. He got picked up on a drunk and disorderly. How did you do with Leeks?"

"I've alerted him that he should steer clear of my case. He's also bringing his son to me for questioning."

Emma's heart lurched. "You're kidding?"

Zac started the car, checked oncoming traffic and entered the fray known as the Saturday-morning rush. "I want to talk to that kid."

"And he's just bringing him to you?" This from Penny who obviously didn't believe it.

"I'm good, Pen, but I'm not that good. I gave him the choice to either bring the kid to me or I subpoena him. Let's see what they decide."

"You're a good man, Zachary."

"Yeah, yeah, yeah. You don't think I know you

played me? Pen, you've been doing this to me since you were twelve. I know you as well as you know me. In this instance, it works in both our favors, but I still can't figure out why I let you get away with this nonsense."

"It's because of my powers of persuasion, big brother." Zac waved his hand, but his grin stretched a mile. "Pick me up at four for dinner with the 'rents. And whatever you do, don't try to sleep with my client."

Emma made a gagging sound and Zac rolled his eyes. "Nice, Pen. Nice."

"Going on record that I've advised you both. I'm not blind and I'm certainly not stupid."

Zac made yapping gestures with his free hand. "Goodbye, Pen."

Emma clicked off and dropped the phone in her lap. "Well, that was…awkward."

"Nah. She's just being Penny. You may have noticed that she likes to stir things up."

"I noticed."

"She's unbelievable. Sometimes I think she'll

give me a stroke, but she's funny as hell. That's the problem with the men in our family. We've spent her lifetime letting her get away with things we shouldn't let her get away with because she entertains us."

"You've created a monster."

"We have indeed," Zac said.

He stopped at a red light and turned to her, his blue eyes twinkling too much for Emma's comfort. Maybe Penny was onto something with that warning.

Plus, all that sibling banter had opened up the emotional sinkhole inside of Emma. Once upon a time, she and Brian had ribbed each other in much the same way. Now? Kind of hard to do with a glass wall between them and thinking about it pressed in on her. *No sadness.* Not now when they were making progress.

Soon things would change. She felt it. Finally, someone would question the victim's boyfriend. "Thank you."

"For what?"

"For pursuing the boyfriend. No one has done that for us."

He stopped at the traffic light on the corner, let out a breath and turned to her. "No problem. Thank you as well. If it weren't for you, the guy would be off the grid. Now, at least, we get to hear what he has to say."

"Yes, we do."

Their gazes locked again and the same crackling silence from earlier returned, making Emma long for something, anything that would offer a distraction.

A car horn blared—distraction granted—and Zac checked the stoplight. Green. "I'm hungry," he said. "You hungry? We can grab a bite."

She shouldn't do it. He *was* the prosecutor on her brother's case. And, well, the towel fantasy still looped in her mind.

When she didn't answer, he gave her an earth-to-Emma look that earned him a swat on the arm.

"We can always discuss your brother's case."

She gasped. "Oh, so dirty. You know I can't resist that one."

"Part of being a good lawyer is knowing your opponent's weakness."

Unbelievable. "Your sister just said that to me! Right before you got into the car. I'm not kidding."

He shrugged. "We learned from the master. Now, where shall we eat?"

Chapter Six

Emma set the steaming hot plate of pasta in front of her last customer and did the can-I-get-you-anything-else spiel. As usual, her feet and body ached from the Saturday-night rush, but she'd go home with a fat wad of cash to plop down on her next tuition payment, so there wasn't a lot to complain about.

From the corner of her eye, she spotted someone sliding into a booth. Really? Closing in thirty minutes and people were still being seated in her section? She headed to the new customer and analyzed the back of his blond head. Couldn't be.

Then he turned sideways and—yep—Zac Hennings. Her heart seized, along with every other part of her. Why would he be here when he'd told her he and Penny would be spending the night at their parents' lake house? *Something's wrong.*

The creepy detective. His son probably fell off the face of the earth. Or they cleared him.

Wouldn't that be her luck?

In the back of her mind, a nagging, paralyzing, incessant fear that sometimes dulled, but never truly vanished, roared with full force. Images flashed through her mind of Brian's bloody body, laid out on a prison floor where he'd bled to death after a prison brawl.

Don't think about it.

Zac shifted sideways and peered over his shoulder, his expression neutral. If he'd at least smile, her fear would go back into hibernation. *Come on, Zac.* But his lips remained...well...flat. He waved, but she stood still, half-terrified to step closer and hear whatever news he had to deliver.

Then, as if sensing her panic, he finally waved her over. She breathed in, ignored her pounding heart and forced her feet to move. Perhaps whatever he had to say wasn't so bad after all.

She stopped in front of his table. He wore navy slacks and a white dress shirt, no tie. Must have come straight from dinner with his folks. Translation: bad news. Horrible news, if he'd driven from Wisconsin to deliver it.

He squeezed her wrist and the connection, all that warm male heat, sparked.

"Everything is fine," he said.

Emma dropped her chin to her chest and breathed. With each exhalation, her pulse slowed a notch and she focused on releasing the tension that had wound her body so tightly. How had she gotten so accustomed to bad news that her mind always went straight there? After a few seconds, her composure restored, she lifted her head. "I got nervous when I saw you."

"I can tell."

She stole a glance at her customers. Everyone was busy eating. She went back to Zac. "I'm sorry. Prosecutors usually bring bad news. I've been conditioned."

"I understand." His lips quirked in a subtle, mischievous way and tingles shot up her arms. "Maybe I can break the trend."

We can't have that. She had no room left for personal sinkholes and Zac Hennings was one giant sinkhole waiting to swallow her up. If her brother's freedom weren't involved, there would be no question that she'd be on this man like nobody's business. But right now, Zac's job was to keep her brother incarcerated.

She could flirt with the charming prosecutor, though. No harm in that. "If anyone can, it's you. Why are you here? I thought you went to Wisconsin."

"I did. We had dinner and I decided to come home. Penny stayed with my folks. They'll all come back tomorrow."

"So you're not here for dinner."

He grinned. "Wicked smart you are."

Oh, that smile—charming and slick and devilish. The man knew his way around a woman's heart. And most likely other body parts as well.

Bad, Emma. Bad.

"I'm here because I don't want you going home by yourself. I'll follow you and make sure you don't have any unexpected visitors."

If ever there was something to make her shamelessly sigh, it was that statement right there. After what had happened to her the night before, knowing how alone she was, Zac Hennings, the guy who could destroy her family, wanted to protect her.

I'm in trouble. Deep trouble.

Nothing about this situation would roll into a happy ending. Her luck didn't hold that long. Not even close. She'd fall for him and he'd wind up keeping Brian in prison. Recovery from that emotional devastation would be unlikely. This, she understood.

Intellectually.

Physically, she craved a connection. Several connections. On an ongoing basis.

Bad, Emma. Bad. She had to get her head together. "Hang on. I have to check this table."

Her customers might have been a lame excuse, but she needed to consider the fine-looking prosecutor with gorgeous eyes and a build she wouldn't mind seeing sans clothing offering to escort her home.

Had Penny told him to do this?

Could be. Or he was just a nice guy, which wouldn't be hard to believe because she'd seen that side of him already. That morning over breakfast—his treat—he'd regaled her with stories of childhood antics involving Penny and her hijinks. Emma had laughed and laughed and laughed and, for the first time in two years, she'd allowed herself an hour of fun. To shut her mind off and not think about Mom and Brian and working on finding a solution for the mess that had become her existence.

Now, tonight, fun time had ended. She had to forget how late it was and the fact that she hadn't been held by a man in an excruciatingly long time.

She checked in with her customers. They were fine. Just fine. Figured. A trip to the kitchen wouldn't have been a bad stalling tactic. Again her luck had gone bad. Back to the charming prosecutor she went. "Sorry about that. Duty called."

"No problem. Do I need to order something while I wait for you?"

"Nah. I'll just tell them you're my ride. The cheesecake is pretty awesome, though, if you want dessert."

"No cheesecake. Anything chocolate?"

Emma propped a hip against the side of the booth and nudged his arm with her elbow. "We have a ferocious brownie à la mode."

Again came the devilish smile. "I love ferocious."

I'll bet you do. Bad, Emma. Bad.

"Okay then. One ferocious brownie for the ferocious prosecutor. Be right back."

One of the other waitresses, Kelly, sidled next to Emma on her way to the kitchen. Work and school and Brian's case had sucked away every last bit of Emma's time, but Kelly had been a constant and the closest thing Emma had to a friend.

Kelly pushed the kitchen door open and held it. "Who's the guy?"

"Prosecutor on my brother's case."

"Shut. The front. *Door.*"

"Truth. I think I have a mad crush on him. He's so flipping hot and I'm a girl who hasn't had a man's hands on me in…a while." She pulled Kelly aside. "I'm crazy, right? Should I feel this way about a guy who wants to keep Brian in a cell?"

"Considering I've never experienced this scenario, I can't really say if you're crazy or not, but yeesh, that guy could melt asphalt. I'm thinking you're crazy if you *don't* sleep with him."

Emma aimed for a laugh, but it came out more like a panicked, hysterical squeak. "This is nuts."

"Don't get nervous. See where it goes. You might wind up hating him."

Yes. She barely knew Zac and getting ahead of herself about the nature of their friendship— or whatever it was—wouldn't help matters. His coming here could be a matter of doing Penny a favor by making sure Emma got home safely.

That's all this was. A guy offering a kind gesture because his sister asked. "You're right. By the time we're done with Brian's case, I'll probably despise him."

Emma nodded to emphasize the point. One solid jerk of her head. Total control. She had it.

Too bad she didn't believe any of what she'd just said.

ZAC TURNED ONTO Emma's street, trying to convince himself that he knew exactly what he was doing. Sure did. He also knew it was an epic— beyond epic—mistake. Bulldozing himself into believing he was a nice guy for getting his sister's client home safely wasn't a problem. That was easy enough. The problem was that under all that chivalry he'd buried a guy who wanted to get Emma Sinclair into bed.

And not just once.

Certain things he couldn't deceive himself about.

All through dinner he'd wondered if Ben Leeks would pay a repeat visit to Emma's. He could see that scumbag doing it just to mess with him. Throw in the chivalrous, but horny guy—the one buried under the professional veneer—and Zac found himself logging the miles back to Chicago.

He parked in the minuscule driveway—a luxury in Cook County—behind her ancient compact and studied the house. He'd always liked the cultural diversity of Parkland. Certain streets had a small-town feel while still being part of the city.

The Sinclairs' small colonial with the sagging covered porch could use more outdoor lighting, but he supposed two women living alone didn't necessarily have the ambition or funds to take on major maintenance projects.

Emma kicked open her car door, held it with

one foot. *I know what I'm doing.* Zac got out, sucked cold air. *Focus here.* She reached over to the passenger seat for her purse and the bag of food from the restaurant and bungled it all. He snatched it from her before it hit the pavement.

"Got it."

"Thanks. My mom wouldn't want her dinner for tomorrow splattered on the driveway."

She locked the car and leaned back on it. The garage spotlight illuminated those luscious brown eyes. Fantastic eyes.

"Do you always bring her food from work?"

"Yep." She shrugged. "She doesn't go out much anymore."

"That's too bad."

"It sure is."

The cold, quiet air whipped around him and he breathed in, let it soak his body and, perhaps, if he got lucky, freeze his lascivious thoughts. He gestured to Emma's unbuttoned jacket. "It's cold. You should button up."

Plus, it would be another layer between them.

The now frozen *and* buried horny guy wasn't too thrilled with the chivalrous guy's suggestion.

"It's just a short walk to the house."

Unless I keep you out here. "Let's get you inside. I'll carry this to the porch for you."

She stared up at him with those eyes that slayed him every time and then a small smile split her full lips. Perfect lips. The top one a hair bigger than the bottom and enough to bring a man down. Horny, frozen guy had big trouble because every inch of him ached to show her how he could put a bigger smile on those lips.

Instead, he gave her a light push toward the door and surveyed the area for a particular detective who had better not be in the vicinity.

Emma climbed the three steps to the wooden porch. Zac spied a loose board on the middle step and stooped to check it. The board flipped up when he pushed on the end. "Hey, you need to get this nailed down. Someone'll break a foot."

"I know. It came loose last week and I haven't had time to deal with it. I'll take care of it."

He stepped over the board and gave Emma the bag. "One of my buddies is a contractor. I'll get him to swing by."

"Thanks, but don't go to the trouble."

"No trouble. He won't mind." He grinned at her. "He owes me."

Emma stared down at the fractured step and sighed. "It sounds dumb, but even getting a stupid board fixed feels like a monumental task."

A gust of wind blew a sliver of hair out of her ponytail and, on instinct, he reached for it. She flinched and he paused with his hand in midair. Her gaze ricocheted to it then back to him and he waited for her to either back away or green-light him. His baser needs hoped for the green light.

I know what I'm doing.

Except they were standing on the porch where any rat-faced detective might be watching. Tree branches smacked against the house and twigs cracked. Zac breathed in and—how about that— she didn't back away.

Green light. What that green light entailed he

wasn't entirely sure, but he'd never been a guy afraid to take a chance. Particularly when it came to women he wanted naked and under him doing wicked things. Slowly, he tucked the loose strand behind her ear. "Houses need maintenance."

"Yeah, but so do people."

Oh, honey.

She slapped her free hand against her forehead, her big eyes horrified. "Wow. That came out so wrong."

Dang, she was cute. Laughing at her, he set his hand on her shoulder and pulled her in for a friendly hug. Maybe it was more than friendly in his mind, but he made sure to keep it PC in case his radar was way off and Emma Sinclair hadn't given him the *go* sign.

His radar was pretty good, though. He kissed the top of her head and visions of her sprawled across his bed, tangled in his sheets, tangled in *him,* filled his mind. Totally cooked. That's what he was. He wanted her—no two ways about it—

and horny, frozen guy didn't much care who might be watching.

She rested her forehead on his chest and rolled it back and forth while he held her there. A few seconds passed. Then a few more. He'd stand there all night. Emma in his arms got his engines firing in a way he hadn't experienced in a long time. He relaxed his shoulders, tried to stay loose and control his raging body. Something was happening here. Something good and hot and satisfying and he always wanted more of anything good and hot and satisfying.

"This is bad," she said.

"Probably."

She snuggled closer and he slid his arm farther around her shoulder, stroking the back of her neck.

"No probably about it, Zac."

"I won't argue, but I generally don't walk away from something this good."

Finally, she retreated. "It's more than good. I'm not sure we should do anything about it, though.

You're the prosecutor on my brother's case. You have the ability to destroy my family. I can't risk that."

He leaned down, got right next to her ear and she stiffened when his lips brushed her skin. "You're convinced he's innocent. Convince me and I'm the guy who puts your family back together."

Again, the tree branch smacked the house and twigs crackled. Suddenly the air was harsh and charged and his skin started to flame. She grabbed a handful of his jacket and pulled him closer. He shifted his head, his lips hovering just over hers. And right then he decided that if they were being watched, he didn't give a damn.

Her breath hitched and she blinked a couple of times. "I guess I'll have to convince you then."

He dipped his head lower, waiting for her to meet him halfway. She lifted her chin and their lips touched. A light brush that made him groan and then he made his move, hauling her in and sweeping his tongue over her bottom lip. She gripped his jacket tighter and pulled him even closer. *Clunk.* Her purse hitting the porch. Still holding the food bag, he wrapped his arms around her and held her close to him, her smaller body molding to the curve of his, while he feasted on her lips, nipping and tasting and wanting more and more and still more.

Something about Emma had buried itself inside him and every minute he spent with her didn't seem long enough.

Slowly, she backed away, but he stole one last nip of that lush upper lip before releasing her. She laughed. "You're a devil, Zac Hennings."

"I'm greedy for sure." He rubbed his hand over her arm. "It's cold. You should go in."

She glanced at the door. "Yeah, I should. I don't necessarily want to, though."

"I know. We have time, Emma."

With the places his mind was going, there'd never be enough time, but he'd figure it out. He wanted her. Job or no job, wrong or right, he'd figure it out.

"Zac, this—whatever it is—will be complicated."

"Yep. I don't know how to get around that. Not going to try. We'll take it a step at a time. See where it goes. Deal?"

She nodded. "Deal."

Chapter Seven

Sunday mornings were always Emma's favorite. Her schedule didn't allow much downtime, and with all the studying she had to do, Sundays were no exception. At least hitting the books could be done in her pajamas with a steaming cup of peach tea.

She sat at the dining room table, tea in hand, flannel PJs keeping her warm and her books sprawled in front of her. If civil liberties and constitutional law weren't the most stimulating reading, she had no one to blame but herself. Typically, she'd be engrossed. Today, though, her mind repeatedly wandered to that soul-scorching kiss Zac Hennings had plastered on her.

Total charmer, that one. But nice. The nice part was the problem. If he'd been a jerk, she could justify hating the prosecutor handling Brian's case. If he'd been a jerk, she could let her anger fester, eat away at her and push her to work harder to free her brother. If he'd been a jerk, she'd have been disgusted by that kiss.

Because he was a good guy, Zac ruined everything.

Above her, a floorboard squeaked. Mom in her bedroom, probably changing the sheets. Another thing that happened every Sunday. Routine kept her mother from thinking too much about Brian.

Emma sighed and went back to her constitutional law book. It was easier than contemplating her mother's state of mind.

The house phone rang and Emma pushed out of her chair to grab the cordless. "Got it!"

She checked the display and saw the too familiar prison phone number. Brian calling. Each inmate paid for calls using his commissary account, which for Emma and her mother, saved a ton on the phone bill.

"Hello?"

"Mrs. Sinclair?"

Not Brian. Throbbing panic shot up Emma's neck into her head. "No, this is her daughter, Emma."

The sound of shuffling paper drifted through the line. "Yes, Emma, this is Trent Daniel."

Brian's prison caseworker. They'd spoken before. Emma's head continued to pound and she pressed her fingers against her temple. *Please, let him be okay.*

"We've had an incident with your brother."

He's not okay. "Is he sick?"

"He was attacked this morning in the prison laundry. The nurse believes he has several broken ribs. We've sent him to the local hospital."

Emma leaned against the counter, thinking prison caseworkers should be required to take classes on bedside manners.

He's alive. She focused on that. Everything else she could deal with.

"Why was he attacked?"

"We're still looking into it. It appears he didn't initiate the fight."

"What hospital has he been sent to?"

"Good Samaritan. They may keep him overnight."

An overnight stay would give him time to rest. She squeezed the phone tighter and, for the first time in years, wondered why their family had to endure so much. But that kind of self-pity never yielded any solutions. Typically, Emma found it a useless endeavor and a complete waste of energy. She relaxed her grip on the phone. "Can we visit him?"

"Yes."

"Thank you." She hung up and stared at the ceiling. Her mother hadn't come down yet. Should she even tell her? Would withholding that information make her a horrible daughter? Or a humane one? Since Penny had taken their case,

Mom's mood had lifted some. This news might send her spiraling back into depression.

And Emma wasn't sure she could handle that. Selfish? Yes. Right now, though, with this latest development, she needed to deal with the immediate problem. She needed to protect herself until she could tell her mother that Brian would be fine.

She scrolled back to the prison number, ran her thumb over the SELECT button and considered her options again. None appealed.

DELETE.

Hoping Mom hadn't looked at the upstairs phone—she'd clear that one in a minute—she charged down the basement steps while speed dialing Penny. It went straight to voice mail. Plus, it was only ten o'clock, so Penny was most likely still at the lake house with her parents. Emma left her a voice mail regarding Brian's condition and that she'd be heading north to visit him.

After hanging up, Emma stood among her boxes of research, wondering what she'd tell her mother about rushing out.

Studying…with a friend. A lie she hoped would be forgiven, but at that moment, standing in that basement, the place where she'd spent countless hours strategizing how to get her brother out of prison, Emma couldn't come up with a compelling reason why she should tell her mother that Brian had been attacked.

She marched up the stairs and found Mom in the kitchen making a fresh pot of coffee. "Hi. Do you want coffee?"

"No. Thanks. I need to shower and run out."

"Why?"

Emma held the phone up. "That was a friend from school. We're studying together. Will you be okay for a while?"

Mom shrugged. "Sure. Take your time. You should go out for something to eat. Have a little fun."

"I could say the same about you."

"Maybe we'll do that this week. The two of us."

Wait. *What?* Had her mother, the shut-in, just agreed to go out for dinner? "Really?"

"Really." Mom glanced around the kitchen she'd called her own for thirty years. "The house is closing in on me."

Emma rushed to her, wrapped her in a fierce hug and a spurt of tears welled in her eyes—what a morning so far. "Thank you. I hate that you stay in all the time." She backed away from the hug. "Let's do it. One night this week. We'll go someplace nice for dinner. How's that?"

"I'd like that."

Headway. Finally. All Emma could hope was that her mother's optimism, like every other time, wouldn't get snatched away.

Thirty minutes later Emma made the left off their street. Her cell phone rang and, not bothering to check the ID, she pressed the button on her earpiece. "Hello?"

"It's Zac."

Had he heard about Brian? "Hi."

"Where are you?"

"On my way to Wisconsin because my brother was injured in a fight and he's in the hospital."

"I know. Penny called me. Stop by my place. I'm going with you. She'll meet us there."

Too much information flew at her and Emma shook her head. Suddenly, she had all these people worried about her brother. A good thing she supposed, but unusual. "Wait. What?"

"Penny called me. My folks are thirty minutes from that hospital. She'll borrow a car and meet us there."

"You don't have to come."

He hesitated. "I want to. Besides, I need to confirm that this incident doesn't have something to do with his case."

"You think someone beat him up because of that?"

"I don't know. I'll find out, though. He's been an exemplary inmate—yes, I checked. Suddenly he's attacked. It's not sitting right."

Emma pulled to the side of the road and parked. *Deep breath here.* Her work on Brian's case might have gotten him injured. God help her.

"Emma?"

"What if it's my fault?"

"It's not. Get to my place and I'll drive. It'll give you a break."

Emma sat quietly, her brain processing the events of the last hour. The hole inside opening wide, ready to claim her. Not only had she lied to her mother, but Brian might have gotten hurt because of her.

"Emma?"

Don't think about it. She shifted the car into gear and pulled from the curb. "I'll see you in twenty minutes."

ZAC FOLLOWED A charging Emma down the hospital hallway where she'd almost taken out a nurse and apologized profusely, but it didn't slow her down. People should know better than to get in her way when she was on a mission. Yeah, he loved that about her.

An armed guard stood outside Brian's room and Emma halted in front of him. After showing her ID, as well as Zac's credentials, they were allowed into the room.

Penny sat in the chair next to a battered Brian Sinclair. Having only seen pictures of the guy from the trial, Zac wouldn't have recognized him. His face looked like a harvesting tractor had torn through it. His bottom lip was swollen and stitched together, the black thread menacing and violent. His right eye didn't look much better. Ugly, black bruises marred the upper lid, the side and underneath.

Emma stopped short and gasped at the sight of him. "Oh, Brian. I'm so sorry."

To his credit, Brian held up a hand. "Don't freak."

Penny nodded her agreement. "The doctor was just in. He has a couple of broken ribs, but that's the worst of it."

Zac stepped around Emma and extended his hand to Brian. "I'm Zac Hennings."

"Yeah," Brian said. "Your sister told me you were coming."

"Zachary," Penny said. "Don't think you're going to interview him."

Cripes. Penny wouldn't give him a break. "Relax, Pen. I only want to know what happened. Then I'll leave the room so you all can talk."

"Fine, but don't pull any funny stuff. I know how you are."

"Pen! I get it. Go back to your lair and let him tell me what happened."

Brian turned to Emma. "They're funny, huh?"

"This is nothing. I can't wait to see them in court." She bit her bottom lip, slammed her eyes closed for a second and squeezed his hand. "I'm so happy to see you. Are you sure you're okay?"

"I'm good. Don't worry. Does Mom know?"

"I couldn't do it to her. Maybe later I'll tell her, but I wanted to see you first." She glanced at Zac, then went back to her brother. "Zac's a good guy. You can tell him what happened."

"I'll keep him in line," Penny cracked.

His sister never gave up, which was probably a good thing. If she had, he'd have to send her to a shrink because something would be seriously wrong. He shook his head at the thought of his sister harassing a psychiatrist. Poor guy would run from the room screaming. *Crazy, Penny.*

"Whatever you're thinking, Zachary, stop it."

He waved her off and leaned against the wall, his body loose and unthreatening, while Emma took the second chair on the opposite side of the bed.

Penny tapped her hand on the bed rail. "Go ahead, Brian."

After boosting himself in the bed, he winced. "I was in the laundry room. That's my work detail. One of the inmates, I don't know who he was, but he was big and sure not happy with me, came up behind me." Brian pointed to the back of his head. "He smacked me on the head with something. Next thing I knew, I was on the floor and he was pounding away at me."

"Any idea why?"

Brian glanced at Emma then looked away. This kid would be a terrible poker player.

Immediately, Emma's eyebrows shot up. "What?"

"Nothing."

"Brian," Penny said. "Tell them what he said."

From where Zac stood, he watched Emma's posture go completely erect. Stiff. *She knows.*

"You can say it," Emma said.

"Don't get nuts on me."

She offered a poor excuse for a smile. "Good luck with that."

Brian nodded. "He knew my name, told me to tell my sister to shut up. That's it."

The words came out fast, like a ticking bomb he wanted to toss. Not wanting to give Emma time to overthink the situation, Zac boosted himself off the wall. "That's all I needed. I'll dig around. See if I can figure out who this guy has a connection to."

Emma spun around to him, threw one hand out. "No. He has to go back to that place. You'll make it worse."

"Hey," Brian said, "I'll live with it."

"Brian!"

"Forget it, Em. Whatever you're doing is shaking things up. If I have to take a beating to get me out of that hellhole, I'll do it. No problem there."

She gaped at her brother—*yeah, she's not happy.* Zac gave Penny the do-something look, but his conflict-loving sister ignored him.

"They'll kill you." Emma's voice rose, the sound breathy and panicked. "Is that what you want?"

"If it means proving I'm innocent, I'll take it. What kind of life do I have? Being locked up for something I didn't do? I liked Chelsea. She was a nice girl and I hate that people think I did that to her...and I miss her."

Apparently, Penny had heard enough. She stood and waggled her fingers at Zac. "I want him segregated from the other prisoners. At least until this is over. Will you back me up on it? It'll carry more weight if the prosecutor agrees."

Zac shrugged. "Of course. We can't have this happening to him. I'll make some calls."

Emma spun around to him, her face, for the

first time, not so pinched and he wanted to think maybe he'd helped with that. "Thank you."

Yeah, he'd helped.

He jerked a thumb toward the door. "I'll be outside. Take your time."

"Zac?" Brian said. "Or Mr. Hennings? What do I call you?"

"As I told your sister, Mr. Hennings is my father. I'm Zac."

"Okay, *Zac*. This has got to be weird with your sister being my lawyer, but thanks."

Weird was probably the best description out there. Zac grinned. "It's definitely weird. But rest assured, she'd like nothing more than to pin me to the courtroom floor."

"Ha!" Penny said. "And you don't want that?"

"Hell, yes. But if you win fair and square, I got no beef." He turned back to Brian. "She's a pain in the butt, but she'll take care of you."

Penny batted her eyes. "Oh, Zachary, how you flatter."

Brian pointed at his sister. "Emma says she's a rainmaker."

That sounded like Emma. "She's tough and she'll make sure your rights are protected. That's about all you can ask for."

Zac touched Emma's shoulder. "Take your time. You're good here until visiting hours are over."

EARLY EVENING HAD almost succumbed to darkness when Emma strapped her seat belt on. While waiting for Zac to turn on the engine, she stared at the neon hospital sign sitting atop the six-story cement building. Ironically, for the first time since Brian's incarceration, she'd sleep tonight knowing her brother would be safe.

She rested her head back, closed her eyes and willed the twinge in her neck away. Every muscle ached. And she still had to face her mother, whom she'd lied to and kept in the dark about her son's condition. Maybe Emma could slip into the house, head straight for her bed and not tell Mom about Brian tonight. The worst of it was over and, at this point, maybe she shouldn't tell her at all.

Did a mother *need* to see the brutal remnants of a beating that had left her son's face swollen and held together by harsh, black stitches? Would she want to see it?

A slow prickle moved up Emma's spine. *What have I done?* Keeping Brian's condition from their mother may not have been fair. *God, I don't know.* A mother would act on basic parenting instincts by going to her child when that child needed care. Emma had stolen that opportunity, ripped it from her mother's hands.

Her stomach twisted and she held her breath. *What have I done?* Panic, slow and vicious and cutting, flooded her system and her heart slammed, just hammered, hammered, hammered at her. Then she felt it. Tears. *Don't cry.* Not here. She bit her bottom lip, squeezed her eyes closed.

Zac backed out of the parking spot and glanced at her. "You okay?"

No. "Yep," she croaked, turning away from him. *Don't let him see.* "Just tired. Long day."

"That it was. Can I get you anything? I'm hungry."

Food. She hadn't had any since that morning. "I guess we should eat." She threw her hands in the air. "Oh, and I'm such an idiot. We should have brought Brian some decent food. What am I doing? I've screwed this whole thing up."

"Hang on." Zac guided the car from the middle of the lot and parked behind a group of empty cars. "Screwed what up?"

Emma hit the window button and sucked in cold air, let it fill her lungs and quiet her battered conscience. She couldn't look at Zac. Not now. He wouldn't understand. How could he? He was Mr. Perfect Family. Mr. I've-got-it-all-together.

Stop. Of all people, he didn't deserve that. If anything, he'd been nothing but helpful. Not many prosecutors would help a convicted man.

"Hey." He rubbed the backs of his fingers over

her cheek, a soft, brushing motion that eased the pounding in her body. "Talk to me."

Even in the dark, she saw it, the compassion in his eyes, the driving need to help. She tilted her head, pressed her cheek against the warmth of his fingers. Being touched was underrated. Or maybe she just hadn't been touched this way in ages. "I rushed into a plan, and robbed my mother of seeing her son outside of prison. Now, I can't decide if I should tell her or just let it be. Either way, I'll probably break her heart. I wouldn't blame her if she was furious with me."

He didn't look away, didn't roll his eyes and didn't judge her. *I could love him.* And, yeah, that was big trouble. Thinking like that would lead her smack-dab into the middle of heartbreak when Zac convinced a judge that her brother should stay in prison. That sinkhole inside her would have a huge payday.

"First off," Zac said, "there's not a right or wrong answer. You had no idea what his condition was. You wanted to protect her."

There he goes, Mr. Perfect. "When I saw that he was okay, I should have called her. I *should* have gone home and gotten her so she could see him."

He dropped his hand from her cheek. "Come on, Emma. How much are you supposed to do?"

Mr. Perfect wasn't so perfect. *Thank you.*

"It's a ninety-minute drive," he said. "By the time you'd have gotten home and back, visiting hours would have been over."

"Then I should have gotten someone to drive her up here."

He let out a harsh breath. If he thought *he* was frustrated, he should climb inside her brain. He had nothing on her.

She unfastened the seat belt and shifted to face him. "You think I'm being ridiculous?"

He turned his head toward her, his blue gaze shooting daggers. "I didn't say that." The edge in his voice, so quiet and controlled, took on a gritty, strangled tone. "If I thought that, I'd have said it. I think you're exhausted and you're over-analyzing."

"And rightly so."

"Wrong!" he yelled.

"Hey!"

He held up his hand, pressed his lips together for a second. "My point is you should give yourself credit for managing an unmanageable situation. There's no instruction manual for this. How would anyone know what the right move is? What it comes down to is you took care of your brother and you saved your mother from worry. Beating up on yourself doesn't help you, your brother or your mother. *That's* what I think."

Emma stayed silent, but folded her arms. Because down deep, tearing away at her, nibbling like a slow-moving cancer, was the urge to crawl across the console and smack him. Just let him have it. She didn't want him making sense of her life right now, trying to fix every damn thing. What she wanted was sleep, and food and a way to forget about her life for a while.

Zac blew air through his lips and rested his head back. "I'm sorry I yelled. I want you to understand that there's no playbook, Emma. No playbook. Don't beat yourself up. You're extraordinary and you don't have to do this alone."

Mr. Perfect returns. "You can't help me, Zac. Your job is to keep him locked up."

"My job is to go into court and prove he did it."

Now they were getting to the meat of the issue. "Do you think he did it?"

He stared out the windshield, drummed his fingers against his thigh. After a minute, he turned to her. "I don't know. Honestly, I don't. I need to talk to witnesses, find the rest of the damn reports that should have been in that box and figure out what's going on with this case."

His being unsure could work for her. Maybe he wasn't committed to finding the real killer, but it was more than she'd gotten from any prosecutor or law enforcement official thus far. "I can help with that."

Light from the dashboard illuminated his narrowed eyes. "How?"

"You told me to prove it to you. I'll give you

copies of all my notes. If Penny wants to use them at trial, we'll have to turn them over anyway, but I'll give it all to you. Even the stuff we don't use."

For her brother, she'd do that. She'd even help Zac sort through it all and explain it to him.

He eyeballed her. "You said it was eighteen boxes. You'll give me all eighteen boxes?"

"I'll give you copies. Not that I don't trust you—you and your sister are the only ones I do trust. Everyone else terrifies me. I need to protect my originals, but I have no problem going over it all with you. I'll show you the inconsistencies in your *rock-solid* case."

Zac grinned at her. "You'll give me everything? Leave nothing out?"

"I have nothing to hide."

He turned and shifted the car into gear. "You, Ms. Sinclair, have a deal."

"Excellent. My brother is innocent. You'll see."

Chapter Eight

Zac stepped into his office carrying his jumbo coffee in one hand and his briefcase in the other. He flipped the light on with his elbow, did his usual scan of the mountains of files stacked in every available spot and wondered if he would ever come in and have an empty desktop.

In a city this size?

Probably not.

He set his cup on the desk and opened his briefcase to sort through the files he'd need for court.

A familiar knock sounded and he glanced up to see Ray Gardner striding toward him. The boss first thing on a Monday morning couldn't be good.

"Hey," Zac said, still pulling folders from his briefcase. "What's up?"

"What's the story with Ben Leeks?"

Zac snorted. Of course the detective went to his superiors about Zac's visit. He probably left out the part about his inappropriate visit to Emma. Zac snapped the briefcase closed, set it on the floor and motioned his boss to a chair.

The two of them sat, just a couple of buddies and no bull. "Ray, this is a mess. How these guys got a conviction baffles me."

His boss shifted in his seat. "How so?"

"There's no evidence. I got one half-filled box of files. No GPRs, no witness statements, nothing. I've got Leeks showing up at Emma Sinclair's at one in the morning and telling her to back off."

"He did that?"

"Yeah, I paid him a visit on Saturday and told him to knock it off and to have his son call me. This kid is the ex-boyfriend of Chelsea Moore and was supposedly abusive. They cleared him within hours. What is that? You can add to that Brian Sinclair spending the night in a hospital last night because someone wanted to send his sister a message. You think that's a coincidence? With the gang contacts Ben Leeks has?"

Ray drummed his fingers on the armrest and twisted his lips. A few long seconds passed—nothing unusual for his boss—while Ray mulled over this new information.

"Look," he finally said. "The SA is all over me on this. She got a call from Grossman over the weekend and he's about to blow his top. I need you to make this go away."

Leeks had taken it all the way to the superintendent of police. Zac should have expected nothing less.

"And what? We don't care that the *investigation* was a joke? I'm not saying Sinclair is innocent, but I have questions. I've also got a copy of a security video showing Sinclair leaving a parking garage down the street from the club at 12:37 that night."

Ray's eyebrows shot up. "What video?"

"My sister tracked it down from a witness statement. A witness who was never called at trial, but who was with Sinclair in the parking garage and drove him back to the club. According to the time line, he would have left his friend's car and walked into that alley to murder Chelsea Moore. Is it a solid alibi? Not necessarily. But why wasn't the friend's testimony admitted into evidence? Something is wrong here."

Ray's secretary appeared in the doorway and Zac held his hand to her. Ray angled back, spotted her and stood. "I've got a meeting. Figure out how to make this go away. Quietly. Please."

Someone was on something if they thought this case would go away quietly, especially with his sister in charge. Kicking up a frenzy was her specialty. She'd mastered the art of manipulating that frenzy in her desired direction at the age of ten. She was, in fact, brilliant at it.

His desk phone buzzed and he hit the speaker button. "Zac Hennings."

"Hi, Zac," the office assistant said. "I have Dave Moore to see you."

Dave Moore. The day couldn't have started off any worse. What would he even say to the man? *I'm sorry, Dave, but your daughter's murder investigation was completely botched.*

No way to win this one. Zac checked his watch. An hour before his first court appearance and he still had notes to review. He'd give Dave some dedicated time—he owed the man that much—and then excuse himself.

"Send him back."

Two minutes later, Dave stepped into Zac's office looking like he'd aged ten years in the couple weeks since Zac had last seen him. His thick head of gray hair was neat and gelled in place, but the loose flesh under Dave's eyes told the story. The man was seriously lacking sleep. Zac rose from his chair and extended his hand.

"Zac, thanks for seeing me unannounced."

He waved the comment away and pointed at the guest chair. "Have a seat."

Dave's large frame dwarfed the chair, but he shifted until he found a suitable position. "These chairs never get any better, do they?"

"Not in my experience."

Dave nodded then looked around at the stacks of folders. Oddly, his gaze landed on the unmarked box on the floor. His daughter's box. No way for him to know what was in it, but his focus sent goose bumps up Zac's arms.

"Dave, talk to me. What do you need?"

The detective tore his attention from the box. "I need you to tell me Chelsea's murderer won't walk out of prison. After that Steve Bennett video, the article in the paper and now I'm hearing noise about your going at it with Ben Leeks, I have concerns."

That dog. Ben Leeks had tapped into every available resource. Even the grieving father.

Zac sat back, his squeaking chair adding to the aggravation of the morning. "I did have a conversation with Leeks. He made an inappropriate visit to Emma Sinclair. This is a politically charged case and he's not doing us any favors." *Neither am I with that whole kissing-the-defendant's-sister thing.* Total mess all around. "I'm working this case, Dave. I'm looking at witness testimony, reviewing evidence, talking to the PD, but I want to be honest with you. There are problems."

Dave's eyes went sharp. "What kind of problems?"

"A serious lack of an investigation for one. I should have a mountain of evidence. I've got half a box. But I promise you, I'll figure this out. Your daughter deserves that and I'll give it to her."

"You think we locked up the wrong guy? That because she was my daughter, the case was fast-tracked?"

Zac wasn't about to tell a detective that his buddies behind the blue wall had manipulated evidence to gain a conviction. "I don't know yet. He was convicted. Something swayed the jury. I've got the trial transcripts on the way. I'll study everything and if Brian Sinclair deserves to be where he is, he'll stay there. I can promise you that."

"But you're wondering."

"I have questions. I won't lie to you. If Sinclair is innocent, the person who did this to Chelsea is walking around. Neither of us wants that. Right now, I need to talk to the Leeks kid and see what was up with his relationship with Chelsea."

Dave nodded. "I'll make sure that happens."

"Don't. I've already spoken to his father about it. He knows I'll subpoena the kid if I have to. For now, I need you to not be a detective working your contacts. I need you to be Chelsea's father. If Brian Sinclair gets a hearing on this new evidence, I want to walk into court with everything aboveboard. No cops cashing in favors. My sister, who's representing Sinclair on the PCR petition, will tear us apart if there's a whiff of impropriety."

"Sinclair did it, Zac. I can feel it. We've gotta get him for good. My wife is a wreck and I don't know what to tell her. We need it to be over."

This poor guy. His daughter murdered, his co-workers screwing up the investigation and now his family would have to go through it again. How the hell was the man supposed to cope? "I'm sorry this is coming back. I give you my word that the investigation will be solid. By the time I'm done, there won't be any questions."

The detective stared at him for a long minute, then, with great effort, pushed himself out of the chair. "I know you're the best they've got. I appreciate what you're doing. If you need my help, let me know."

Zac waited for Dave to leave, then picked up his desk phone and dialed Emma. Her files were looking like the Promised Land right now. Pressure had never been an issue for him. Part of him lived for it, the rush of energy, the high that came with battle. For him, it meant euphoria. It meant walking into court and decimating the opposition.

Except he had a thing for Emma Sinclair—also known as the opposition. Worse, she might be right about her brother's innocence—damned if he knew—and it would rock a city already rife with political scandals.

Emma picked up on the third ring.

"Hey, Emma."

"Hello, *Zachary.*"

And wow, that spot-on imitation of Penny was bizarre. Zac laughed for the first time today. *Hell.* Another reason to like her. She made him laugh when everything else gave him an ulcer. "You sound just like her. That's nuts."

"I've been practicing. I can't help myself. She's such a character. How are you?"

"I'm good. You okay?"

"You mean after my trip to psycho-land last night?"

He laughed. "I wouldn't call it that, but yeah."

"I am. I had decent sleep. I'm taking your advice and not beating myself up. What's done is done."

Good for her. "What did you decide about your mom?"

"I didn't tell her. Brian's caseworker just called

and he's on his way back to the prison. I didn't see much point in telling my mother now."

"Probably the right move."

"I hope you're right, *Zachary*." She laughed. "I'm sorry. I'm punchy. I've been studying constitutional law since five."

On top of all this, she was a law student keeping up with her studies. "Oh, that's good stuff right there."

"You think?"

"I know. We're talking about the foundation of our country. Constitutional law is all about our society's fundamental relationships."

"Well," Emma said, "since you're an expert, you can help me study for my test on Friday."

"Anytime. I love that subject. I know it every which way. That's not what I'm calling about, though."

"Somehow, I figured that."

Well, shoot. He should have called her this morning to check on her. That would have been the right thing to do after the day she'd had yesterday. The lines of separation on this case were starting to shift. To *blur*. Regardless of his feelings for Emma, he had to focus on winning. On giving Dave Moore and his family the answers they deserved. "When can I get a look at your files?"

"*Zachary,* you're so forward."

Again, he laughed. *Those shifting lines are nonexistent now.* "You don't want to go there with me, Emma. I take dirty talk to a whole new level."

Silence. Yeah, he thought so. So did his erection. *Dammit.* "The files?"

She cleared her throat. "Right. The files. After the copy machine gets here."

"What copy machine?"

"The one your sister insisted on because she refuses to let you take one slip of paper from this basement. She told me she'd have a copy machine sent over so you can make dupes of whatever you need."

Leave it to Penny. At least it was coming out of her budget and not the state's.

"That'll be convenient," Zac said. "When is it getting there?"

"She said sometime today. I'm off tonight if you want to come by."

He checked the calendar on his phone. Pickup basketball game at seven. He'd have to skip that. "Tonight works. I'll swing by after work. I'll even bring dinner."

"Perfect. Bring enough for three. My mom will be here."

EMMA SWUNG THE front door open and found Zac standing on the other side juggling his briefcase and enough pizza to feed a small army. She grabbed the two pizza boxes from him. "Zac, we're only three people."

"I figured there'd be enough for leftovers."

Leftovers. How incredibly sweet. "Well, don't just stand there. Come inside."

He stepped into the living room and looked around. Just days ago his sister had been in the exact spot. Of course, her reasons for being there were about defending Brian whereas Zac's were about prosecuting him. No one had ever accused Emma of leading a boring life.

She led Zac to the kitchen where she set the food on the despised and scarred Formica countertop. One day, they'd rip it out and give their homey kitchen the update it deserved. Some of Emma's most cherished moments—family breakfasts, her father's corny jokes, fresh-baked cookies with Mom—occurred while sitting in this kitchen. No wonder her mother refused to give up the circa-1985 table. The table held memories of a life that no longer existed. A life stolen by death and injustice.

Emma pointed to the floor where Zac was about to step. "Don't trip. The linoleum is coming up."

Being the fixer he was, he squatted and pressed it back into place.

"Thanks, but it'll only come up again. It's one of the projects on Brian's to-do list when he comes home. He's handy that way."

Zac nodded, seemingly unmoved by her declaration that Brian would be coming home. "Where's your mom?"

"She went out for a bit."

"Doesn't want me here, huh?"

Might as well tell him the truth. Smart man that he was, he'd figure it out anyway. "It's not that. I told her you were a nice guy."

He cracked a grin. "Did she call you a liar?"

"No. She loves Penny, so it wasn't hard for her to believe. I think it's more about not wanting to like you."

"Come again?"

Needing a minute to align her thoughts, Emma set one of the pizza boxes on the table and flipped it open. "I think she's afraid she'll like you and then you'll keep her son in prison."

Kind of like me.

"There's an angle I never considered."

"I'm not sure how she'd reconcile those two things. She's used to life kicking her to the curb, but that might be too much."

Emma grabbed a couple of plates from the cabinet, found the necessary silverware and arranged everything on the table. Yes, she was stalling and they both knew it. "What do you want to drink? Pop, iced tea? I could probably scrounge a beer from the back of the fridge, but I can't vouch for how long it's been there."

His lips quirked and Emma got that little rush—the zipping heat—that had distracted her too many times over the last few days. "Pop is good. Thanks."

She busied herself with two cans of pop while Zac pondered the pizza. "We can eat and then head downstairs. No food down there. I once bumped a bowl of chili and it splattered all over my notes. It's now a no-food zone. And if you drink down there, it needs to stay away from the work space." She grinned. "Evidentiary rules."

"You're cute, Emma Sinclair."

"Compliment me all you want. You're still not bringing food or beverages into my work space."

"I'm fine with your rules. They're good ones."

Pizza devoured, Emma loaded the dishwasher

and led Zac to the basement. A sudden whoosh filled her head. For the first time, she'd be allowing the enemy to see her notes. That alone was a monumental step and she took comfort in knowing she trusted this man enough to give him access to her life.

At the bottom of the stairs she flipped the wall switch and her corner work area lit up.

His eyes feasted on the boxes. "Yowzer."

"It's the Operation Sinclair command center."

The copy machine Penny had sent over stood in the farthest corner beside the boxes, a bright white beacon against the gray cement wall. "I hope you know how to use that copy machine because it's got way too many buttons for me to figure out."

"It's probably the same one they have in their office. I'll show you how to use it." He stepped over to the boxes—*three high, six across*—and scanned the labels. "Emma, this is unbelievable."

"I told you I had eighteen boxes."

"Seeing them is different. I've seen teams of detectives that can't gather this much information."

Teams of detectives didn't have a brother in prison and a mother stranded in the grip of depression. "When it's personal, you work harder. Where do you want to start? I have three boxes of statements from people who were at the bar that night." She pulled one of the boxes off the stack and set it on the long folding table she used as a desk. "This is the first set. There are two others."

Zac lifted the top and spotted the individually marked folders. He lifted a few out and opened them. "You have statements like this from each person?"

"Yep."

"Emma, you'll be an amazing attorney."

All the hours she'd spent in this basement, poring over notes, studying cases, organizing files, not one person had ever said that to her and her chest locked up, seizing in a way that stole her breath.

"Thank you. Coming from you, that's tremendous praise." She waved her hand toward the files. "I found all of Brian's friends who were at the club. Then I found Chelsea's. Some of them weren't thrilled to talk to me. I understood, but I kept at it and eventually I found more and more people who were there. Oh, and I ran an ad in the paper looking for witnesses. I'll never do *that* again. You should have seen some of the crackpots."

"Tell me you didn't put your phone number in the ad."

"No. I set up a dedicated email account. Still, I came across some nutcases."

"I'm sure."

"It was worth it, though. I have over two hundred statements."

Again, he shook his head. "I'm in awe. Too bad Penny snatched you as *her* intern. I could use you."

"Except you're the enemy."

He glanced at her, his gaze suddenly serious. "Right now, I'm just a guy trying to figure out what the hell is going on with this case." He picked up a file. "Where do I start?"

Someone on the other side wanted to help. After all these months of contacting the press, stalking attorneys, *begging* for assistance, she still had trouble believing it. "Well, *Zachary,* that depends on what you're looking for."

"The white shirt is bugging me."

She knew exactly which shirt he was referring to. "The one Brian wore that night?"

"Yes. The witness said the man in the alley wore a white shirt. It was March. I checked the temperature that night. Forty-three degrees. Did Brian wear a jacket?"

Her answer wouldn't help them. She knew it, but it was the reality and something she'd learned not to fear. At this point, there were too many other things worth fearing. "He said he left it in the car. It was a nice leather one and he didn't want to take it into the club."

"Blows that theory." Zac unbuttoned his shirt-sleeves and rolled them up. "I guess I'll dig in."

"Thank you."

"For what?"

Their gazes met and held for a long minute and Emma felt that same heat, that yearning to do something she shouldn't do. *Bad, Emma. Bad.* "For everything. For taking the time to figure this out."

He shrugged. "It's my job."

"Not all of what you've done is your job. Bringing me home the other night, driving me to the hospital yesterday." *Kissing me.* "You didn't need to do those things."

A slow smile eased across his face. "Maybe I have a thing for the defendant's sister."

Feeling a little playful—and when was the last time that happened?—Emma fanned herself. "I might have a thing for the prosecutor, too."

"Could be fun."

"Could be an awful mess."

They both knew it—no sense ignoring it. Awkward silence was shattered by the furnace kicking on. Not necessarily a bad thing, considering that they needed a distraction from exploring their mutual attraction.

Zac tapped a finger on one of the folders. "I'll find out what happened with Chelsea, but you may not like the outcome. You need to be ready for that. My sister is a great lawyer and she's got my father to help, but…"

Emma held her hand up, then dropped it again. "I know what you're saying. You don't want us to get our hopes up."

"I don't want you to get hurt."

Silly man. She was an ace at hurt. Hurt had no teeth left except when it came to him. That she wasn't so sure about. "Zac, all we have left is hope. If it doesn't go our way, we'll deal with it. The Sinclair family, unfortunately, is used to disappointment."

The electric charge of moments ago roared back and his gaze swept over her. From head to toe, he quietly took her in and the stillness, all that power and control he was so good at unnerved her. She wiggled her fingers and he glanced down at her hands.

I don't know what to do.

Finally, he stepped toward her, pulled her against him and kissed the top of her head. "This is complicated."

Complicated. Good word. Under her cheek, his heartbeat thumped and Emma settled there, enjoying the much-missed comfort of a man's arms around her. She fiddled with the button on his shirt, flicking her finger back and forth. They could just stand here like this for a while. A few more minutes was all she wanted.

He backed away. Of course he did. When had she ever been lucky enough to get what she needed or craved out of life? She looked up at him and those baby-blue eyes gazed down at her. Gripping his shirt, she pulled him down and kissed him. Softly at first, but when he tightened his hold, something inside her shifted. For once, she—the caged twenty-six-year-old woman who hadn't experienced affection in...well, she wouldn't dwell on how long—didn't feel like rushing to the next item on her to-do list. Particularly with Zac's hands finding their way under her sweater to bare skin and—*yes*—her body detonated. A veritable explosion of fire and loneliness and yearning all bursting free, frying her from the inside.

She pulled him closer, clutching his shirt, hanging on while he nipped at her lips, making her want more and more because—oh, it had been so long since she'd felt this scorching need to be close to someone. Had she *ever* felt this?

I'm boiling. Not good. The loneliness, the neediness. It was all too much. *Overload.* Her skin got tight. *He'll destroy me.*

She gripped his shirt harder, willed her mind to silence. *It'll hurt when he leaves.* No good.

With one last peck, Zac backed away. "You okay?"

She darted her gaze over his face. Such a fine face. Strong and angular and oh so touchable. "No." *Really, Emma?* What was wrong with her?

But Zac smiled that million-dollar smile of his and ran a hand over her hair. Just a gentle touch that let her know he understood her brand of kooky. And didn't that do her in completely? Somehow, she'd found safety in this man. Or maybe all the nights alone had simply made her think she'd found safety.

"I'm sorry. My mind is raging. But I love every second of kissing you. I'm alive again and that's a gift." She tugged on his shirt. "A gift I want a whole lot more of."

He pulled her in again and she rested her head against his chest while he stroked her back. Up and down. Up and down. Up and down. A gentle, repetitive motion that did wonders for her frazzled senses. His chest rose and fell under her head as he let out a giant breath. "I think that can be arranged. Show me your files first."

"Kinky, *Zachary.*"

Stepping back, he shook his head. "Seriously, you have to stop talking like my sister. It's freaking me out."

"You're no fun." She waved toward the boxes—
three high, six across—she was about to let the
prosecution have access to.

And to *her*. In the last ten minutes she'd sliced
her life open and exposed every vulnerable artery
to the enemy. Now she had to prepare for the con-
sequences. But she'd do that later. She smacked
her hands together. "Let's get to work."

Chapter Nine

After hours of reviewing case files and breaking down time lines, Zac knew there was more than thirty minutes when Brian's whereabouts were unaccounted for. From the sudden silence in the basement, he'd guessed that Emma knew it, too.

Brian had left Melody's car around 12:45. His friends all made statements that he was with them, but no one could pinpoint the exact time, at least not until 1:20, when one guy received a text and remembered showing it to Brian.

Thirty-five minutes. Plenty of time for someone to slip out of a nightclub, walk to the alley next door, strangle a woman and return. Zac kept his eyes glued to the witness statement in front of him, not really reading, but not ready to look at Emma yet.

As good as Penny and their father were, those thirty-five minutes would work to Zac's favor. Even with the holes in this case, he could create enough of an argument to satisfy a judge, make his boss happy, give Dave Moore his so-called justice and keep Brian Sinclair in prison.

Assignment complete.

But was it the right thing? For the first time in his career, a career filled with emotional cases that he'd both won and lost, he found himself questioning his own judgment because he wanted to get laid. *Moron.*

Seated next to him at the long folding table, Emma sighed and the soft sound hit him square in the chest. He wanted her, no doubt about it. His problem was that he didn't just want her. He cared for her. This was a woman who'd put her life on hold to salvage the remaining rubble of her family. Emma saw problems as opportunities. Whatever the issue, she found a way to strap it to her back and carry it. What man would be crazy enough *not* to want her?

Which was why his reasonable self—knowing he was messing with something he shouldn't mess with—turned tail and ran. *Hell with it.* He grabbed the bottom of her chair and rolled it closer so he could snuggle her neck. "It's 10:30. I should go."

Rather than shoo him away, she tilted her head, exposing her neck. "Yes, you should. My mother will be home any second now. I feel like a sneaky teenager. You're a bad boy, *Zachary.*"

"Ah, yes, my sister's voice."

Emma cracked up. "Sorry."

But Zac kissed her, one of those long, slow ones that would torture him long into the night. "So, yeah, I'm going to leave before I try to convince you to hop into bed with me."

She waggled her eyebrows. "Right now, sailor, that wouldn't take much convincing."

"How you wound me."

"You'll survive, I'm sure." She gestured to the

stack of folders he'd set aside. "Do you want me to copy everything in those folders for you? I have a class in the morning and then I'm working the lunch shift. I'll have time after that."

He stood up, grabbed his jacket from the back of the chair and slid it on. "Emma, between work and school, you don't have time to be copying notes. I'll send someone over to do it."

"If it'll help my brother, I'll make the time." She went up on tiptoes and kissed him quick. "Besides, I don't want anyone touching my notes. Not that I don't trust you. I do, but accidents happen and something could disappear."

"You don't have to explain to me. I'm a prosecutor with half a box of evidence. Thank you. How about we go through more of this stuff tomorrow? At my place so your mom doesn't have to leave."

Emma bit her lip, looked down at her feet. "I don't know."

Losing her.

"My sister will insist on armed security for the

folders, but I'll talk to her, convince her that I won't abscond with evidence."

Laughing at him, she looked up and rolled her eyes. "She let you in here, didn't she?"

"Maybe she trusts me after all. How about you? Do you trust me?"

"I let you in here, didn't I?"

He shrugged.

Again, she bit her lip. Indecision was a wicked thing. Finally, she shook her head. "I don't want to do anything stupid. Penny is our hope in all this. Then you come in here and kiss me and I think *Penny who?* That bothers me."

He tugged the front of her shirt. "If it makes you feel better, it bugs me, too." He grinned. "I like kissing you, though."

"Such a man."

"Can't help it. What do you say? Tomorrow night?"

"You'll behave?"

"Realistically? Probably not."

She laughed and the sound lit something in him that would keep him awake the whole damn night.

"Then I guess I'll see you tomorrow," she said.

He leaned over and, already blowing his quest to behave, kissed her again, nibbled those lush lips. Her lips could drive a man insane, thinking about all the uses for them. "I guess you will."

AFTER ZAC LEFT, Emma checked on her mom who had parked herself at a friend's house and was now on her way home. If nothing else, it was good for Mom to get out some. Emma stacked the folders to be copied on the tray table she'd set up next to the copy machine. Starting on them now would save time in the morning.

Plus, she was too keyed up to sleep. Intimacy, she decided, was a beautiful thing. She'd gone too long without this tingly, happy feeling that came with having the right man touch her.

Zac Hennings, for many reasons, might not be Mr. Right, but he was definitely Mr. Right Now. Setting aside the fact that he was the opposition, he was a good man. A good man willing to look beyond the surface of her brother's case when others had turned away.

She stood in front of the copy machine and picked up the first folder. The one containing her notes about the white shirt testimony. Zac seemed a little obsessed with the white shirt. She wished she could have told him Brian hadn't been wearing white that night. That it was all some dumb mistake and that he'd worn blue. The case would have fallen apart if he'd simply worn blue. Such a simple thing could have changed it all. *Why didn't you wear blue?*

No use dwelling on it. Emma opened the folder and read her notes. Witness at end of alley. Saw man coming toward him. Moved on. Her gaze shot left again.

End of alley.

On a moonless night. She remembered that from her investigation. She'd checked on it. It had, in fact, been heavily overcast that night. Dark. Really dark.

End of alley.

Emma dropped the folder and papers scattered in a blanket of white at her feet. "Oh, my." She scooped up her phone, charged upstairs to her bedroom and grabbed one of her white work shirts, a jacket, her purse and keys and flew out the door.

As she ran to her car, she scrolled her contacts for Zac's number. Hopefully he'd meet her there because only stupid women walked in dark city alleys late at night. Emma wasn't stupid. At the same time, this mission could only be done in the dark. The call went straight to voice mail and she hung up. She'd call back from the road.

Once en route, she tried Zac again, but the phone beeped. On the line. She'd leave a message. "It's Emma. On my way to the crime scene to check something. Can you meet me there?"

She drove past Magic where even on a Monday people headed in for a night of partying. A sign with bright red letters indicated dollar draft night so the college kids probably showed up en masse. On the busy main street, cars stacked up at the traffic signals. Half a block down, one of the many city bridges spanned the Chicago River, its lights twinkling against a black sky. She stopped in a no-parking zone at the alley entrance and slapped her hazards on. A cabbie flew by, sitting on his horn and the sharp blare grated up her neck.

"Take it easy, mister," she muttered.

Her phone whistled and she checked it. Voice mail from Zac. She punched the button and his deep voice filled the car. "It's me," he said. "Three minutes out. Wait for me."

Another car whooshed by and she chomped her bottom lip. Sooner or later a cop would move her along. The dashboard clock blinked. Another two minutes and Zac would be here.

Someone knocked on the passenger window. The banging sent blood slamming through her and she swung her head sideways. One of the bouncers from the club jerked his thumb. "Lady, you gotta move."

Emma grabbed her purse, jumped out and shut the door before a passing car ripped it off. She worked her way to the curb and stared up at the massive security guy. "Hi. I'm an investigator." *Investigator?* "Working on a murder case. I need to check something in the alley. Real quick. Promise." Digging into her purse, she fished out a twenty. "Will you keep an eye on the car a minute?"

"Lady—"

"Two minutes. That's all I need."

The bouncer glanced around, snatched the twenty out of her hand and nodded. "Go. Fast."

"Thank you." From the passenger seat she grabbed the white shirt and headed into the alley.

So much for smart girls not going into dark alleys alone. Desperate measures, right? Besides, Zac would show up any second.

Still, she headed in, moving slowly at first, letting her eyes adjust to the blackness. The only lights were halfway down the alley over two adjacent doors on each building. From the street behind, a car horn honked, then screeching tires. Prickles coursed up her arms and even in the cold, the air felt hot against her. The sides of the buildings pressed in and her eyes darted left and right. Anyone could be hiding here and she wouldn't see him. *Take a breath.* She turned back. No bouncer.

Was this what Chelsea heard right before she died?

For that matter, Chelsea must have had a reason for coming into this scary place alone. Emma would have to study her files for any pertinent info on that. Yes. Focus on the case.

A light wind blew and the stench of ripe garbage forced her to scrunch her nose and gasp. A garbage container was somewhere close.

She stopped in the approximate area where Chelsea Moore spent her last moments. Between the rancid smell and visions of the young woman trapped against the wall, her throat being crushed, Emma's stomach churned.

Closer to the lights now, she spotted the offending container overflowing with garbage. Probably the weekend pile-up. On her right was a thin electrical pipe running up the side of the building. Not a great test subject, but it would suffice. Emma shoved the white shirt into the gap. There. All she had to do was run back to the alley entrance and verify that the shirt could be seen from there.

Behind her came the squish of rubber on damp pavement. *Zac.* She started to turn and a hard shove sent her sailing into the brick building. Her cheek smacked the cold, rough surface. A ripping sensation tore into her and her lungs froze. No air.

Stupid girl.

"You don't learn, do you?" a guttural voice whispered and the sound, so low and ugly and hard, sent a violent burst of panic up her throat.

She opened her mouth to scream. Nothing. Paralyzed. The man's hot breath snaked over her skin and she gasped. *Don't let him win.* Her eyes watered. She blinked, fought the tears seeping free. *Breathe, Emma.*

Chaos and fear whirled through her mind. *Turn*

around. Look at him. Her minimal self-defense lessons flashed into her head. If she could get to his throat or his eyes, she'd have a chance. She shifted, tried to spin, but he shoved her against the wall, his bigger body leaning into her, crushing her.

"Help!" she croaked.

Her attacker laughed and pushed his body further into hers. "You wanna die right here like Chelsea Moore?"

Vomit heaved into her throat and she gagged, swallowed it back. *Someone, help me. Should have waited for Zac...Fight. Don't let him win.* Messages and warnings came in a rush, battering her oversensitized system, shredding what was left of her nerves.

Elbow.

She jerked her elbow back and connected—his arm maybe—but it skidded off.

And then she got mad. Mad enough to show this jerk that she wouldn't be an easy victim. Not ever.

"No!" she hollered, her voice suddenly coming to her aid. *Thank you.*

"Emma!" Zac from the alley entrance.

"Here."

The pressure from the man's disgusting body eased up and she sucked in a breath, all that rancid air flooding her lungs. She turned and swung. Nothing there. A shadow sprinted to the back exit of the alley. The clomp of shoes—Zac's dress shoes—sounded from behind her.

Catch him. Knowing Zac would follow, she gave chase.

"Did you see him?" she hollered over her shoulder.

"No."

She had to find him, see who he was and what he knew about Chelsea Moore.

Zac caught up to her, his longer legs making the task easy. "Emma, hang on."

He grabbed her arm and halted her, but she struggled against his hold as her attacker fled. *No. No. No.* "He's getting away."

She yanked free and ran to the far end of the alley, looking both ways. *I've got to find him.* Crushing disappointment, like rising water, overtook her, stole her breath. *I blew it.* Whoever it was, he'd disappeared. "No!" Her echoing rage bounced off the surrounding buildings and she squeezed her fingers into tight, knuckle-popping fists. So much pressure.

Then Zac was next to her, sliding his arms around her and pulling her in for a hug so fierce it sparked that same heat that she'd felt earlier. *Concentrate, Emma.*

"What happened?" he asked.

Not wanting to be babied—who needed that?— she elbowed away and stared into the blackness where her attacker vanished. *Damn it.* She shook out her hands, let her aching fingers recover. "He pushed me."

Zac set her back and squeezed her arms. "Mugger?"

"No. He said…"

What *did* he say? *Think, Emma.* She spun

around, pointed. She'd been standing there, right there, shoving the shirt into the pipe and then— bam—he'd shoved her. As she stared at the spot and envisioned the attack in her mind, his voice came back to her, low and mean and vile, and she focused. *Think*. The words tumbled in her brain and she separated them, gave them order. "He said, 'Do you want to die like Chelsea Moore?'"

"Oh, honey. I'm so sorry. Did he say anything else?"

Zac hugged her again, holding her against him and the warmth of his bigger body drew her closer. After all the battles she'd fought alone, someone wanted to take care of her.

"Yes." Emma backed up, waggled her hands as the words came back to her. "He said, 'You don't learn, do you?'"

In the darkness, Zac's arm moved. "I'm calling 9-1-1."

Emma stilled his hand, kept him from dialing. "Wait. We must be getting close to something someone doesn't want us to find. He followed me here."

"Lady!" The club's security guard. "You gotta move this car!"

"Be right there!" She turned back to Zac. "The bouncer was rushing me. I paid him twenty bucks. That's why I didn't wait for you."

"What *are* we doing here?"

"Lady!"

"We're coming," Zac yelled back, his voice carrying an unmistakable don't-screw-with-me message.

Grabbing his hand, Emma dragged him back to where she'd shoved her shirt. The stingy light illuminated them and she pointed at it. "I wanted to see if we could see the white from where the witness was standing. Maybe that's what's bugging you about the shirt."

For a full ten seconds, he stared at the shirt then turned to the alley entrance. He grabbed her hand. "Come with me."

The two of them strode back to her car, Emma

double-timing to keep up. At the entrance, Zac whirled around. She did the same thing. Behind them traffic whooshed by as they gazed into the darkness where the meager light showed two doorways. Only two doorways.

No white shirt.

ZAC KNEW THAT someone had to stand in the alley with that shirt on. Except it was Emma's shirt and he wasn't about to send her back in there.

"Dude," the bouncer said. "You gotta move these cars. It's a fire lane."

But Zac was distracted by a white shirt he couldn't see. He studied the bouncer. Big, but not huge. A size or two bigger than Zac.

I'm wearing a white shirt.

Following Emma's lead, he peeled a fifty from his money clip. "My name is Zac Hennings. I'm a Cook County Assistant State's Attorney. We're investigating the homicide that occurred here two years ago."

"The cop's daughter?"

"That's her." Zac held the fifty between two fingers. "This is yours if you'll put my shirt on and stand in the middle of this alley. That's it. Fifty bucks. It'll take two minutes."

Come on. Take the money. He needed to see for himself if that shirt was visible from his vantage point. If not, he'd haul the detectives back here and prove to them that it couldn't be seen from this distance. Something they should have done and something the SA's office should have confirmed.

Dammit.

Zac didn't know what to feel right now. Frustrated with shoddy investigating? Sure. Terrified that his case was coming apart? Definitely. Worried about Emma? Absolutely.

And yet, if the evidence fell apart, it would help her. But this was his job and his boss wanted to save face for the SA.

The bouncer glanced at the club's doorway. *Losing him.* Zac flicked the fifty at him. A second later, the bill was gone. Zac hurried out of his jacket and Emma took it from him, watching as he stripped down to his undershirt. Did she have to do that? Talk about a distraction. Cold air blasted his bare skin, bringing his mind back to his task rather than taking his clothes off in front of a woman he'd like to see do the same.

Emma held his jacket up and he slipped his arms into it. "Thanks." He went back to the bouncer. "Go halfway down the alley and stop."

While the security guard made his way down the alley, Zac glanced at Emma and the red scrape he'd failed to notice when they'd first come out of the alley. His face got hot and his typically reined-in temper flared. *Should've gotten here faster.* He'd never considered himself a chest-pounding alpha male, but another man putting his hands on Emma made him want to gut someone.

And he was the prosecutor.

What a mess.

He propped his finger under her chin and tilted her head up. "You've got a scrape. Did he hit you?"

"No. He shoved me into the building, and my cheek crashed into the brick."

"I'm sorry." He leaned down, dropped a kiss on

the spot. "I'm sorry you're hurt and that I didn't get here sooner. We have to be more careful."

She squeezed his wrist. "I should have waited. Next time I'll wait."

"This good enough?" the bouncer yelled from the middle of the alley.

"Yeah. You're good. Hang there a sec." Zac took a few steps left, separating himself from Emma. He had to focus on his job, on not letting his growing feelings for this woman sway his judgment. He stared into the blackness. Nothing. He took two steps closer to the alley entrance.

"You remember where the witness was standing?" he called to Emma.

"He said he was walking past the club on his way to the garage so he'd have been on the sidewalk and crossing. You're probably closer than he was."

Then she was next to him, her energy an electric current zapping him hard. The two of them looked into the black mouth of the alley, not seeing a thing.

Now Zac had a problem.

Chapter Ten

After her eight o'clock class, Emma drove to the North Side to meet Penny at Stanley Vernon's home. Mr. Vernon, the star witness for the prosecution, had identified Brian as the man wearing the white shirt in the alley and Penny wanted to shake him up.

Considering Emma informed Penny of the white shirt test the night before, Penny, being Penny, sensed blood gushing from Zac's case. If they could get Mr. Vernon to recant, Penny felt sure their request for a post-conviction relief hearing would be granted and Brian would have a chance at a reversal.

This meeting was crucial to their effort. Emma

breathed deep and squeezed the steering wheel. Moisture from her hands made the surface slick and she scrunched her nose. *Relax. Let Penny do the talking.*

On her first pass around the city block, she spotted the spunky lawyer in her pink coat—not hard to miss—waiting for her two doors down from their intended target. Remembering Zac's cross-eyed irritation from the morning he'd spotted that coat gave Emma a moment of respite from the giant knot between her shoulders. *Popsicle Penny.*

As siblings went, Zac and Penny were a funny pair. Clearly, their affection ran deep, but she imagined that when they fought, they fought hard.

Being attorneys, Emma assumed they were used to the conflict, but she wasn't sure she could face her brother in court. Her protective instincts would kick in and she'd worry about beating him.

Zac and Penny didn't have those issues. Not with their kill-or-be-killed instincts. They craved the slaughter. The *win.*

Emma found a parking space half a block from Mr. Vernon's home. The short walk and fresh air would help clear her mind for the conversation about to take place. Part of her wanted to run screaming from this encounter. In a few moments, she'd have to face the man who'd helped tear her family apart. Maybe, at the time, he'd felt he was simply doing his civic duty, but she now knew that he'd lied on the stand.

And she had proof in Zac's white shirt.

Emma stepped onto the sidewalk, straightened her trench coat and ran a hand down the front. She'd opted for a knee-length navy-blue skirt and light blue sweater for this meeting. Not too lawyerish or bold. She took one step and—*whoops*—her thin heel sank into the crack in the sidewalk, the soft dirt holding her hostage. Terrific.

Outside of special occasions, she never wore heels and now knew why. She slid out of the shoe and squatted to free it.

"What?" Penny called from four houses down.

"Keep your panties on. My shoe is stuck."

Obviously enjoying the show, Penny shook her head. "I do love you, Emma."

"Yeah, whatever."

She plucked the shoe free and used a tissue from her purse to wipe the heel. Upsetting the Vernons by leaving a trail of mud in their home certainly wouldn't help their cause. Her shoe clean once again, she half walked, half jogged to where Penny was standing. "I'm sorry. I hate heels. I'm never good in them." She pressed her hand to her head where a sudden throb nearly split her skull. *I'm a wreck.*

Penny squeezed her arm. Not hard. Just a light, reassuring gesture. "Relax. I've got this. You sit and look sincere. The guilt alone will kill this guy."

"I'm afraid I'll screw up. What if he refuses to talk in front of me?"

"Then I'll send you outside, but I have a hunch that won't happen. When I tell him we tested the white-shirt theory, he'll take one look at you and cave. Trust me. We'll be fine."

Emma smacked her eyes closed. Penny, the only lawyer in town with enough faith, or maybe it was nerve, to take their case, needed her and she was having a meltdown. Not smart. The knot in her shoulders tightened and Emma rolled her head side to side. She could do this. Hadn't she interviewed over two hundred witnesses? Some of whom had literally run from her, but she'd kept at it, hour after hour. She'd hounded them. And persuaded them to talk to her.

I can do this.

She opened her eyes and jerked her head. "Thank you. And, no pressure here, but my brother's life is in your hands."

"Oh, please. As if *that* would work on me." She linked her arm with Emma's. "Let's eat this guy alive."

Lawyers.

They climbed the four brick steps leading to a two-story, aluminum-sided, single-family home. The porch columns looked recently painted and Emma felt a pang of guilt over the neglected maintenance on her mother's home. There was always so much to do. Penny knocked on the front door and the repetitive thunk refocused Emma.

I can do this.

A plump woman with bleached-blond hair— maybe fiftyish—opened the door. She spotted Penny in the popsicle coat and smiled. Then she turned to Emma. The smile evaporated. *I can do this.*

Penny shoved her hand out. "Mrs. Vernon? I'm Penny Hennings. We spoke on the phone."

The woman's gaze slid back to Penny and her smile returned. "Yes. Hello. Come in. My husband will be right down."

"Thank you."

Penny followed the woman in, but swiveled to Emma and crossed her eyes. Emma cracked a smile, thankful her lawyer's energy was strong enough to handle any grim task.

Mrs. Vernon ushered them into a sitting area at the back of the house. Three large windows of the converted porch overlooked a patch of yard with wisps of early-spring greenery. In the summer, it would be a quiet, comforting spot for reading. Not that Emma did much pleasure reading anymore. Who had time?

The woman motioned them to the upholstered love seat, offered them coffee and went about all the niceties required when guests arrived. A valiant effort, but Emma imagined that their presence wasn't all that welcome.

While Mrs. Vernon tended to the beverages, Penny sat erect and unmoving, her hands in her lap. Even in a motionless state, her crackling energy suffused the room. Pink coat and fair-haired beauty aside, this was a panther ready to pounce.

A man entered the room. Mr. Vernon. Emma recognized him from court, but he was thinner now, somehow smaller than he'd been when she'd seen him during Brian's trial. As if life had beaten a few inches off him. She could relate.

For a moment, she remained buried in the shock of seeing him. His testimony had decimated her brother's future and torn away another chunk of her family. *Don't go there.* Penny popped off the love seat, slapped the glamour girl smile on her face and stuck her hand out.

"Hello, Mr. Vernon. Thank you for seeing us. So kind of you." Emma unglued herself from the chair and stood. "Allow me to introduce Emma."

Funny how she left off the last name. Mr. Vernon held out his hand. His gray-blue eyes narrowed a bit, not mean, more questioning. Within seconds his eyebrows lifted. Recognition complete. The poor man made an effort to smile, but it came off stiff and unyielding.

Apparently, Emma wasn't the only one feeling the pressure.

"Nice to meet you, Emma."

Liar.

"You, too, sir."

Liar.

Penny smacked her hands together. "Shall we sit?"

"Yes, please. My wife offered you a drink?"

"Yes, thank you." Penny settled back into her

seat and waited for Emma and their witness to park themselves. "Mr. Vernon, as I mentioned on the phone, we'd like to ask you a few questions about your testimony."

His gaze shifted to Emma, then back. "I'm not sure how much more I can tell you."

How about that you lied? Emma clasped her hands in her lap, determined to keep her trap shut.

Penny reached into her briefcase for a legal pad. "Do you mind if I take notes?"

"That's fine."

The Popsicle Penny smile, all sweet and gooey, broke loose. "Thank you. I'd like to ask you about the white shirt you said you saw on the man in the alley."

Vernon's throat bulged from a swallow. Interesting.

"Sir, we did a re-creation in the alley."

"I don't understand."

Penny flipped her palm up. "A man wearing a white shirt stood in the alley where Chelsea

Moore's body was found. We did this at night, of course."

Mrs. Vernon entered the room with two coffee mugs and handed one each to Penny and Emma. "Thank you, ma'am," Emma said.

Penny set the mug on the table next to her. "Mr. Vernon, I don't mean to be argumentative and I'm not questioning what you saw—" She smiled that sweet-girl smile that had probably destroyed an army of men. "Well, maybe I am. You understand. I need to clarify the details."

"What details?"

"About the shirt. When we did our test, the man wearing white could not be seen from where you said you stood."

"How can that be?"

"I'm not sure, sir. Are you certain of your location? Or perhaps the man in the alley was closer than you thought."

Mr. Vernon glanced at Emma, then shook his head. "No."

Liar.

Trap shut. Emma sipped her coffee, but oh, how she wanted to rage and scream at him to tell the truth. Her brother's future had been ripped to shreds, *stolen,* and this man dared to sit in front of her and lie?

Her hands trembled and, fearing a spill, she set the mug down, then flexed her quivering fingers. A total wreck. But she'd keep quiet and let Penny handle it. For once, someone else could do the dirty work. Right?

Right.

Except someone else hadn't lived with her mother night after night and listened to the never-ending weeping. Sometimes, on the really rough nights, the weeping turned into sobs and Emma shoved earplugs in because she couldn't stand the torture her mother was enduring. Even now, eighteen months after her younger child had been found guilty and shoved in a cage, Mom still cried herself to sleep.

Emma bit her lip. *Let Penny handle it.* But, but, but how hard would it be to tell the truth?

She couldn't do it. Couldn't sit here simply accepting the lies. *Nope, can't do it.* "Mr. Vernon, are you a parent?"

Ever so slowly, Penny inched around and gave Emma the wide-eyed, don't-make-me-kill-you glare.

"I have three children," Mr. Vernon said.

Emma nodded. "Sir, I know you wanted to help find a murderer by testifying and I appreciate your willingness to do that."

"But?"

"But my mother has a son in prison. If someone were to accuse one of your children of a crime, a crime that would send them to prison for the better part of their adult life, wouldn't you want that person to be sure of what he saw?"

"I am sure."

Emma gripped the sofa cushion and squeezed. "I don't think you are, sir. I stood outside the alley myself last night and couldn't see the white shirt. There were two of us. Neither of us saw him."

Penny scooted forward. "Mr. Vernon—"

He held his finger up. "Are you accusing me of lying?"

Uh-oh. Penny would skin her. "No, sir. I'm trying to figure out what it is you saw."

Penny set her hand on Emma's arm. Okay. Point taken. Emma was shutting up now.

"Mr. Vernon, I'm sure you're aware that a video has surfaced that shows one of the detectives confessing to pressuring witnesses." Penny dug in her briefcase for her phone. "I have a copy of the video if you'd like to see it."

"Don't need to."

"No?"

"No."

She dropped her phone back in the purse. "That's fine. Let's talk about the night the police questioned you. You were shown a series of photographs, correct? Six, if I'm not mistaken."

"Yes."

"After that you were taken to view a lineup, correct?"

Vernon shifted away from Emma and her pulse

kicked. The man couldn't even look at her. His body language all but screamed it. This was getting good.

"Yes."

"And you identified Brian Sinclair?"

"Yes."

"Mr. Vernon, how many of the men in the photo lineup were wearing a white shirt?"

Vernon opened his mouth then stopped, tilted his head as if stumped.

"Sir?"

Go, Penny.

"Just one."

Penny made a note and Mr. Vernon's eyes bounced every which way. God, she was good.

"I see. The only one in a white shirt was Brian Sinclair?"

"Yes."

"And at what point did the white shirt enter into the conversation?"

Again, Mr. Vernon shifted, his shoulders slumping a bit. His entire body seemed to fold and Emma's heart banged. *Please, let this be it.*

"Before the photo lineup," Mr. Vernon said. "The detectives asked me if I remembered the person in the alley wearing a white shirt."

"So the detectives suggested that to you?"

"Well, they asked me."

"And you remembered that."

Vernon licked his lips. "I identified the kid. That's who I saw in the alley." He turned to Emma. "I'm sorry for your family. I wouldn't wish it on anyone. I can't help you, though." He stood. "Thank you for coming. I'll show you out."

Emma gawked, her mouth literally hanging open while Mr. Vernon hurried from the room. Just that fast, everything had derailed. How?

She glanced at Penny who shoved her notepad back in her briefcase then held her finger to her lips. "It's okay," she mouthed.

Emma nodded. What else could she do? At this moment, she had to be a professional. She couldn't be a grieving, heartbroken sister. She followed Penny through the house and nodded at Mr. Vernon as she strode out the front door.

"Well, that was a bust," Emma said when they reached the sidewalk.

She glanced back at the house where she'd blown her chance to help her brother. Penny charged in the direction of Emma's car. She must have been parked in the same general area.

"Since when are you so negative? Buck up, sister. I told you we were about to climb Everest. We're barely at the first camp and you've got a long face."

Oh, and now she was gonna start? "Excuse me? You forget who's been doing this climb for two years now."

"Yeah, without a Sherpa. I'm the Sherpa. I'll get your butt to the top. You can't give up." She stopped, hefted her briefcase higher on her shoulder and folded her arms. "That was our first go at him. I didn't expect to walk out with a confession. We presented our case. We rattled him. Now we let him stew on it. He'll cave. Did you see the way he looked at you when you gave him that parent speech? Girlfriend, you're gonna be an amazing lawyer."

Wasn't that what Zac had said? Coming from these two, with their lineage, she might even start to believe it.

"I thought I blew it."

"I'll admit that you scared me for a second, so let's stick to the script next time, but it worked. Obviously, he's a man with a conscience. My guess is that at this very second he's dialing his detective buddies wanting to know if they manipulated him."

She spun around front and started walking again. "I love this job, Emma. It's such a rush."

Emma did her half walk, half run thing to catch up. Penny had to be one of the tiniest women Emma had ever laid eyes on, yet she moved like a ninja. "I think you're insane."

"You're not the first to accuse me of that. Here's my car. Just so you know, I'm sending an investigator to talk to Chelsea's ex-boyfriend."

"Really?"

"Yep. I figure after his father paid you that visit the other night and with Zac pressuring him from the SA's side, it couldn't hurt to get under the kid's skin. Who knows if anything will come of it? I'm guessing not because Daddy will tell him to keep his lips buttoned, but, hey, you never know. It would be interesting to know if he was the one in that alley with you last night."

Emma closed her eyes, let her mind drift back. "I'd remember his voice. Mean. Nasty."

"Good. That's important. You need to be careful, okay? My dad thinks you need protection. I tend to agree."

"I can't afford that. I'll be careful. No more stunts. I promise."

"We could probably help with the expenses for protection. I'll ask my father."

Absolutely not. There was only so much charity she could handle. "I'm not taking money from you. You're doing enough."

Penny fished her keys from her briefcase and hit

the UNLOCK button. "Think about it. Great work today. Don't worry. This is all good. Just hang in there with me, okay?"

Emma nodded. "I will. Thank you."

"No. Thank *you*."

"For what?"

"For making me look like a superstar, of course. And whatever you do, don't have sex with my brother."

Emma's feet fused to the ground and it had nothing to do with a stuck heel. *What?*

Penny opened her car door and tossed her brief-case in. "I know my brother and he wants to jump you. A sexual relationship between the two of you would be emotional warfare. He wants to win as much as we do. If he wins, you lose. If you win, he loses. Either way, one of you gets hurt."

ZAC KNOCKED ON his boss's half-open office door and stuck his head in. "Got a sec?"

Ray looked up from the document he'd been reading, dropped his glasses on the desk and sat back. "Whatcha got?"

Aggravating his boss required privacy so Zac shut the door.

"Oh, hell. You're gonna ruin my day, aren't you?"

A little bit, yeah. Zac sat on the miserable love seat against the wall. Not that the place had room for a love seat, but he supposed being the boss meant Ray wanted something no one else had. Something like a love seat in an office already crammed with an overstuffed bookcase.

"I went to the alley. Where Chelsea Moore was murdered."

Ray groaned.

"Yeah. We got a witness saying he saw Brian Sinclair in that alley wearing a white shirt. Last night I had the bouncer from the bar stand in the alley in a white shirt."

Ray groaned louder. He understood exactly where they were headed.

"I think we need an investigator on this. My sister is all over the shirt."

The SA's office had its own investigative bureau, which handled specialized offenses, including official misconduct. They were the impartial eyes of Cook County and if ever a case warranted an impartial eye, it was this one.

"Hang on. You told your sister?"

"No. Emma Sinclair was with me. She told my sister."

Ray jerked his head. "What?"

Go easy here. The boss popping his cork wouldn't help. "She called me last night with this theory about the white shirt. She wanted me to authenticate her experiment." *Close enough to the truth*. "I met her there. The shirt couldn't be seen. If I know my sister, she's already leaning on the witness trying to get him to recant."

Ray grabbed a notepad and pen and started writing. "We've got the video and the shirt. And let's not forget Ben Leeks's stunt with Emma Sinclair," Zac's boss said.

"No GPRs in the case file. What there is of a case file."

More notes. "Right."

"Ray, these detectives phoned it in. There are

too many holes. They latched onto Brian Sinclair and made it fit. Right now, I'm not sure the kid did it."

Ray snapped his head up. "Whoa."

"I'm not saying he didn't. I'm saying we don't have enough to know. If I was working Felony Review and the cops came to me with this case, I'd say they don't have the horsepower."

Ray slapped his pen down and ran both hands through his short black hair. Tension Zac hadn't felt all that often filled the cramped office. He waited. Talking now would be suicide.

The baseboard heater clunked. Zac ignored it. He refused to move. Finally, Ray gave up on his hair and set his hands on the desk, his fingers tapping the memo he'd abandoned. "All you had to do was make this go away. Now you're telling me you can't."

A sharp stab hit the back of Zac's neck. *What the hell?* Busting his tail on this and his boss is miffed because the case is a stinker. Forget about the guy they locked up, the one who might be innocent. "Am I supposed to concoct evidence? Talk to the detectives and see what the hell they were thinking by not writing up any reports?"

"There's gotta be something."

Sure. Right. No sweat. Zac grunted. "This case is a disaster. And, no, I can't make it go away."

"It's been less than a week. How can you know that?"

Unbelievable. "Come on. I know a dog when I see one. This is a *crippled* dog."

"Then work it harder. Make something happen."

For the first time, a picture of his boss formed. A picture Zac didn't like. One that pitted a political system against a twenty-two-year-old kid convicted of murder. Sickness rolled in his belly. What was wrong with these people that they let politics dictate the outcome of trials? He was far from an idealist, but this sizzled him.

Zac shot out of his chair and threw the door open. It hit the wall hard and Ray stared at it, his cheeks turning a flaming red.

"Don't you walk out of here."

To hell with that. "I think we're done."

"Hennings!"

But Zac kept moving. No sense stopping. He'd just alerted his superior that they had catastrophic problems with a murder conviction and the only advice he'd received was to make it go away. As if it would be that simple. As if he'd be able to live with himself knowing they put this kid away on bogus evidence. Well, he couldn't. Call him the last good guy standing, but if his boss wanted to reprimand him, demote him, so be it. He wasn't about to risk his law license by rigging a case.

Chapter Eleven

Emma climbed the stairs to Zac's second-floor apartment and a sudden case of the jitters sent her pulse twitching. She paused in the center of the staircase.

Run.

Being here with him—alone—was probably a mistake. *Probably?* No question about it. This was a colossal risk. After the scorching kiss-fest a few days ago she might have lost a few brain cells. Either that or her body and its lack of male attention had taken over and decided not to heed Penny's warning about Zac.

But hey, they were adults capable of controlling

themselves. She glanced at the folders tucked in her right arm.

It's fine.

She hefted the shopping bag in her other hand to her wrist, grabbed the knob at the top of the polished oak railing and pulled herself up. She loved these old houses with all the dark wood trim. The door to his apartment opened and there stood Zac, wearing black track pants and a T-shirt that hugged his shoulders in all the right ways. He never wore tight clothes, but somehow they always molded to the long, lean muscles that spanned his upper body. His blond hair was wet and combed back, revealing those perfectly an-gular cheeks and—yep—Emma needed a man.

Pronto.

So much for not thinking about it.

Total mistake.

Zac grabbed the stack of file folders from her. "Something wrong?"

Everything. What was she doing letting herself get involved with the prosecutor on her brother's case? Brian's only chance in eighteen months and Emma was hormonal about the hot prosecutor. She should march right down the stairs and out the door. No harm done. Except she couldn't discount the kisses they'd shared. Those were definitely something.

She hadn't slept with him, though. Even if the way Zac Hennings moved turned her liquid and made her fantasize about things they could do together.

"Emma?"

Walk away.

She handed him the bag of takeout. *Too late now.* "Sorry. Thinking too much."

"I know the feeling. Come in." He shut the door behind her and set the folders on the side table. When he turned back to her she spotted it, the hardness in his eyes, the taut cheeks and locked jaw. Standing this close, his raw energy, primal and predatory reached her, sending a burst of heat to her core.

Is it hot in here? "Bad day?" she asked.

"My day stunk."

"Sorry to hear that."

He stepped closer, staring down at her for a second while his gaze moved over her face, stalled at her lips and then went to her trench coat. Zac had something on his mind and—being the smart girl she was—she could make a good guess as to what it was.

Walk away.

"You feel that?"

Sure do. She swallowed. "Um—"

"It's crazy. The minute I get close to you, it's an explosion."

He slipped his hands into the neckline of her coat, pushed it off her shoulders and down her arms, and caught it before it hit the floor. He tossed it over the living room chair.

But his eyes were on her lips again. Her stomach dropped and heat surged and—*wow*—she got a little woozy. *Two rational adults.*

He dipped his head closer, teasing, testing to see if she'd meet him halfway.

No. She stepped back, hunched her shoulders. "We're not behaving. Either one of us."

It shouldn't have been wrong. Not when it felt so right and good and natural. Since Brian's nightmare began, she'd been denying herself the basic human need to be touched. To be loved. And now she had her chance. For Emma. Not for anyone else but her. For once, only she should matter. *I need a man.*

This man.

Zac straightened, shook his head. "You're right. I'm sorry. My fault." He banged his hands on his head. "I'm all screwed up. I know it's wrong, but I want what I want."

He wasn't the only one. Maybe just once what would be so bad about that? No strings. Even if she'd never been the no-strings kind of girl, she'd make this one exception. *I want what I want.* That want pushed her to her tiptoes, stretching toward him, angling her head until her lips hovered close enough to feel his breath on her face. She waited, hoping he might stop her.

I need a man. Screw it. She clamped her hand on the back of his neck and hauled him closer. His lips slid across hers and she mangled his shirt in her fist while Penny's warning blared in her head.

Penny who?

She focused on the feel of his perfect lips on hers and pressed closer, needing the contact, the feel of his body against her. So long she'd been without affection, without the caress of hands. Then her skin caught fire, every inch sizzling, and she wrapped both arms around his waist and pulled. How close could she get? She wasn't sure, but she knew it wasn't enough. Enough of this didn't exist. She'd always want more.

He broke away and kissed across her jaw. Emma lifted her chin, exposing her neck.

"Atta, girl," he said.

"Penny says we shouldn't have sex."

"Penny is a pain in the ass."

More kisses and his hands moved under her blouse, his thumb stroking her belly. *Penny who?*

"You could be right about that."

Apparently that was all he needed because he lifted his head and gave her his million-dollar country-club smile.

She glanced down as he worked the buttons on her blouse, one button, two buttons, three buttons. And then her shirt was open and his hands were on her breasts, detouring as they moved to push the blouse off her shoulders, those fantastic fingers moving down her arms until the shirt was off and Emma's chest hitched.

He wanted her. Somehow she believed it was more than sex. Maybe it was the gentleness of his touch or the brief hesitation that gave her a chance to follow Penny's orders, but it was there, urging her forward. *Penny who?*

He gave her a playful push toward his bedroom. *One of us will get hurt. Most likely me.* Right now, though, with all this crazy lust roaring inside her, she'd risk it. All this time she'd taken a backseat to everyone else. If she could have one night that was all hers, one night to forget all the problems and heartache, one night of ecstasy, she'd live with potential heartbreak. When it came to a broken heart, she was a pro.

In the bedroom, Zac yanked his shirt off and tossed it. Light from the hallway threw shadows and she watched the shirt sail through the air and land on a high-backed chair in the corner of the room. She reached for him, giving herself a minute to explore the planes of his chest and shoulders. Yes, it had been too long. Closing her eyes, she let the moment drift and stretch and settle in her mind so she'd always remember.

"You okay?" he asked.

"I'm great. It's…" Her voice trembled and she stopped. *Don't lose it now, Emma.*

He backed away, cupped her face in his hands. "What?"

"Fun. It's fun. And I've been without fun for a long time."

"Fun is good." He nudged her backward and her calves smacked the edge of the bed.

She sucked in a breath, her arms flailing as she flew backward and landed with a whoosh.

The prosecutor wanted to play. From the bed, she placed her foot on his belly and pushed. "You're going to get it for that, *Zachary.*"

"Bring it on, Emma. Bring it on."

Slowly, he lifted her foot and ran his hands along her leg, his long fingers skittering over her jeans as they made their way up. So good. Inside, little by little, she came apart, abandoned all control.

He settled one knee on the bed and went to work on the button at her waist.

"I've got it." She flicked the button and worked the zipper down.

Again, Mr. Prosecutor went to work, removing her jeans, those dangerous hands slowly moving over her bare legs. He glanced up and the slant of light from the hallway illuminated his face and the slow, easy smile quirking his lips. Her chest hitched again. She was gone. So gone.

He'll destroy me.

But she didn't care. She shot to a sitting position, clamped her hands on the waistband of his pants and shoved. "Get these off."

Then something happened, like an eruption of energy, the air around her crackled and her skin tingled and snapped and she breathed in just as Zac kissed her, his tongue doing magic things to her. Needing the contact, Emma dug her fingers into his back.

Zac broke away, flipped her over and unhooked her bra. She flipped over again, still in her underwear, but letting him see her. Even in the dark, she saw that gleam in his eye. "Get naked, Zac. I'm a chick in need."

He cracked up, but did as he was told. How she loved a man who followed directions. He reached across her to his bedside table and his erection poked her leg. *Wow.* It had definitely been a while since she'd felt *that.* The crackle of foil drove away the silence and Emma tried not to think too hard about him keeping condoms in his bedside table. Or the women who'd been here.

Not going there.

Within seconds, he was back to her, trailing kisses over her chest, those luscious hands moving over her breasts and stomach and she slapped at the bed, squeezing the blanket. Surely she would die from all this attention.

She opened her legs and watched him slide between them. God, he was gorgeous. She wanted this, wanted him. Grabbing his cheeks, she pulled him to her and kissed him. Long and soft and then he pressed into her and she gasped. Too good.

They moved together, her locking her legs around him and gliding her hands over his back, then his face and chest, and when he settled himself on his elbows and kissed her again it was all too much. She'd been alone for way too long.

She held on and moved with him, their bodies in perfect unison, and then her stomach clenched and she sighed. Zac licked behind her ear, teasing her. He got as good as he gave because the muscles in his back tensed under her hands and he picked up his pace, racing, racing, racing until her mind whirled and her body turned frantic while she held on, wanting to prolong this moment before it all went away.

Too late.

Her world exploded into enormous flashes of light and ecstasy. She focused on breathing, enjoying the long-denied release of a good, healthy orgasm. Her world wasn't the only one exploding. Zac collapsed on top of her, his breaths coming in heaving bursts while she ran her hands over his back, along the quaking muscles.

"Heck of a way to end a rotten day," he said.

"I'll second that."

After a few moments, he rolled off her, taking all the warmth with him, and a blast of cold sent goose bumps up her legs. Zac lifted his arm, an obvious invitation for her to snuggle into his side. She wouldn't complain. She curled into him and ran her hand through the wispy blond hair in the center of his chest.

"Emma Sinclair, somehow I didn't figure you for a snuggler."

"Usually I'm not." Loneliness did that to a girl. "So you figured right."

He nibbled her neck. "I'm a snuggler."

Oh, this man is a total destroyer. But she wrapped her arms around him and squeezed because it all felt so right. So effortless.

Perfection.

Don't go there, Emma. Perfection didn't exist. At least not for her. She eased her hand over his hip, drew tiny circles and loved the feel of being so close. "We have food out there. We should eat."

"There's food, too?"

Smarty-pants. "Yes, there's food. And then we have work to do, so no funny stuff."

Finally, with great effort, Zac rolled away. Part of her hated it, wanted him to stay close, let her feel loved a bit more. When had she turned into such a needy person?

Maybe since she'd been without affection for so long.

Who knew? She watched Zac gather his clothes

and slide into his pants, already wondering if they'd do this again.

"Emma, quit looking at me like that or you won't get food. I'll keep you in this bed all night."

Promises, promises.

ZAC TUGGED HIS shirt on and from outside the bedroom, a cell phone chirped. Good distraction before carnal thoughts coaxed him back to bed.

"That's my phone," Emma said.

"I'll grab it for you. In your coat?"

"Yep. Pocket."

He left the room in search of the phone and to give his brain a minute to catch up to what just happened. If there were any more ways to annihilate his career, he wasn't sure he could find them.

But, yeah, Emma Sinclair was worth it. She had to be because he'd never crossed the line when it came to his job. Right now, he didn't care, didn't anticipate caring in the near future, either.

More of Emma was what he wanted.

He retrieved her phone, grabbed the bag of food

and headed back down the hall. He'd heat up dinner while she got dressed. Give them both a little privacy. By the time he stepped into the bedroom she'd already slipped on her blouse. "Don't get dressed on my account."

She swatted at him and bent to pick up her jeans. "Yeah. Whatever, mister."

"Can I turn on the light?"

"Sure."

Zac flipped the switch, flooded the room with light and found Emma with her eyes closed. She slowly opened them and he imagined lazy mornings watching her roll out of bed. *Easy now.*

He handed her the phone and she checked the screen. "Oh, this is funny."

"What's that?"

"It's a text from Penny. What timing." Using her thumb, she hit a button. "Oh. Oh, wow."

This should be good. He waited, wondering if she'd share whatever news Penny had sent. Was that fair? To wonder? To expect it?

Hell if I know.

After a second, the silence morphed into awkward and he held up the bag. "I'll nuke the food."

Emma finally lifted her head. "Zac?"

"Yes?"

"She got a call from Ray Gardner."

Son of a gun. If he were being taken off the case, he'd have been told. Maybe not. Ray had been pretty steamed at him earlier. Zac waited, the silence tearing his brain to shreds. "Ray is my boss."

"He's assigning an investigator from the SA's office to Brian's case."

Air flew up Zac's throat and came out in a whoosh. If it was relief or satisfaction, he didn't know. Either way, his boss had redeemed himself. Zac leaned against the doorframe and stared at Emma's face, where a tentative smile appeared. Her eyes filled with tears and she blinked them away.

"It's okay to be happy," he said. "You've worked hard for this."

She lifted the phone then let her hand drop

again. "I know. I just can't believe it. Someone is listening."

"And you made it happen." He held up the bag. "I'm on the food. Take your time."

He turned from the doorway, hoping she wouldn't press him on what he knew about the investigator. In short—and overdue—order he had to separate his job and this case from his feelings about Emma. It was all too intertwined and…muddy.

"Zac?"

He popped his head back in the bedroom and she held the phone up. "Did you have anything to do with the investigator being assigned to this case?"

"I may have suggested it as a precaution."

"You think my brother is innocent."

Trouble. Part of him wanted to tell her he agreed with her, but the truth was, he didn't know. The prosecutor in him wanted to believe the jury got it right and hadn't convicted an innocent man. But he'd also been an ASA long enough to know that, sometimes, justice got sidetracked. Things went wrong. Innocent people went to prison.

He tapped his hand against the doorframe and stared into her big, hopeful eyes. "I think there are inconsistencies with Brian's case that need to be looked at."

If she was disappointed, she didn't show it. Nothing moved. No slumping shoulders, no dramatic sigh, no pinched eyebrows. Nothing. Emma Sinclair, rock star.

Finally, she ran her hands over her legs and drummed her fingers. He should say something. Even if he wasn't ready to admit that Brian might be innocent, he should say *something*. But that was the tricky part.

"Emma—"

She held up her hands and attempted a brief smile that screamed of indecision. "It's okay. You're a prosecutor. I know what your job is. And thank you for suggesting the investigator. It's more than anyone from your office has done since this nightmare began. That means a lot to me. By the end of this, you'll see that Brian is innocent."

For her sake, he certainly hoped so.

Chapter Twelve

After her morning class on Wednesday, Emma headed to her mother's favorite Italian restaurant, a little hole-in-the-wall near the United Center. With her crazy schedule, she and her mom hadn't managed to arrange a dinner out together, so they'd found a sliver of time to squeeze in lunch.

As she drove, Emma turned up the volume on the radio and sang along. At the traffic light, still wailing, she glanced at the car next to her and found the driver, a young guy wearing a baseball cap, howling at her. *Hey, whatever.* She threw her arms up and wiggled them. Still laughing, he shook his head and waved her off. Fun stuff, that. It had been too long since she'd allowed herself to lighten up, to keep from being so serious about every darn thing.

Blame it on the orgasms—as in multiples. Thanks to one Zachary Hennings, whom she couldn't seem to stop thinking about today. A total stud.

Bad, Emma. Bad.

Emma made a left on a tree-lined street where the homes, in typical city fashion, had roughly six inches of space between them. She found a parking space a block away from the restaurant and called it a done deal.

Not a bad day for a short walk. She tightened the belt on her coat and faced the unseasonable cold. Even if the temperature hadn't made it out of the forties yet today, the sun's warmth poured over her. She'd take it after the vicious winter they'd had. Above her, a few birds chirped and the clear blue sky stretched as far as she could see. She stopped, tipped her head up and the damp smell of early spring tickled her nose.

Two years of her life had slipped away, two

years of not taking a few seconds to enjoy a pretty day or belt out a song. Two years of being smothered under the blanket of a wrongfully accused brother.

As was typical of her life, the piercing shriek of a police siren interrupted her moment of grateful appreciation. Out of curiosity, she spun toward it and spotted a Chicago squad car near the corner, where he'd made a traffic stop. A car that looked suspiciously like her mother's. *Oh, come on.* Mom finally leaves the house and she gets pulled over? And for what? The woman barely drove the speed limit. If anything, she'd be cited for driving too slowly.

To be sure, Emma moved closer and—yep—that was her mother in the driver's seat. The officer hadn't gotten out of his car yet and as Emma got closer, she found her mother digging through the glove compartment, probably looking for her registration and insurance card. Emma pulled off her glove and tapped the passenger side door. Her mother flinched, glanced up and slammed her hand against her chest.

"Open the window," Emma said.

From the driver's side, her mother lowered the window and Emma stuck her head in. "What happened?"

"I don't know. He just signaled me over."

"Did you run the light or something?"

Mom scoffed. Perhaps the timing stunk, but Emma laughed. She had to. "Sorry. Stupid question."

The cop finally heaved himself from his car, slipped his cap on and headed their way. Emma backed out of the window and stood tall. "Hello, officer."

"Step away from the car, please."

He wore a light jacket, obviously padded with a vest underneath. In this town, any cop would be nuts not to wear one. This was her home, but it was still a city and cities had gangs and drugs and guns that could steal a life.

"This is my mother." Emma jerked her thumb down the street. "We're meeting for lunch."

"Yeah, fine. Step away from the car." The cop's nasty gaze focused on her and he pointed to an area in front of the car. "Move. Now."

What the heck? A second officer—this one younger and not as tall, but bigger-chested—got out of the car and walked toward her. "Ma'am, step to the side."

Mom leaned over to the passenger side and spoke through the window. "Emma, it's fine."

The second cop puckered his lips, glanced at the other cop and gave a subtle nudge of his chin.

Emma eyeballed them both. "Why are you pulling her over?"

"Broken taillight. License and registration, please."

Emma angled around the second cop to check the taillights. If Mom had a broken taillight, it had just happened because they were fine this morning. Both taillights were intact. She pointed to the taillights. "They're fine."

The first cop wandered to the back of the car and stared at the driver's-side taillight. "This one is burned out. I saw it when she made the turn."

"Mom, hit the brakes."

Both taillights lit up. Emma gave the first cop a hard stare, daring him to argue with her. "It seems you're mistaken."

The cop shrugged. "She must have a short in the wiring. Better get it checked before she has an accident, *Emma*."

And the way he said her name, sarcastic and taunting and drawing out the m's. She jerked her head back and then came the "aha" moment. Her mother didn't have a broken taillight. Her mother had a daughter making the CPD look bad. Clearly, they didn't like that because not only had they pulled her over on a trumped-up violation, they'd suggested that her mother might have an accident.

That, Emma would not stand for. She threw her shoulders back, held her head higher. "Are you threatening us?"

The cop placed his hand over his chest in mock horror and Emma thought her blood would seep clear through her pores. She'd like to climb over the car and pummel him. Just beat him senseless for being an idiot.

"Ma'am," the second cop said to her mother from the passenger side, "we'll let you go with a warning today, but you need to get that light checked."

A warning. They'd given the warning all right.

The second cop stepped around Emma and headed back to their car. She watched him for a second and zeroed in on his name tag. *Collins.* Gotcha. She brought her attention back to jerk number one. She hadn't gotten close enough to catch his name, but she had his partner's. She'd find them.

Jerk number one tipped his hat. "Enjoy your lunch, *Emma.*"

With all the crime happening in a city the size of Chicago, these creeps had nothing better to do than harass a widow whose son was in prison, wrongfully convicted.

Despite the brisk air, hot stabs punctured Emma's skin. They weren't harassing her mother, they were harassing her. First it was the detective coming to the house and now this. From the curb, Emma watched the lights on top of the police car move down the street. That crazy detective and his friends were trying to scare her by targeting her loved ones, by letting her know they could find them wherever they happened to be. Well, guess what? She was out of loved ones.

Emma stooped down and looked at her mother through the still-open window. "Are you okay?"

"I'm fine. I don't understand what happened with that taillight. I'll have to have it checked."

Part of Emma wanted to tell her mother that it wasn't about the taillight, but what was the point? Why give her another thing to worry about when she was finally finding her way out of depression? Giving her mother any questionable news might send her back to that joyless, mind-numbing state she'd been in for too long.

Emma opened the car door and slid in. "I'll take care of it. Let's find a parking space and have a nice lunch. Maybe we'll even have a glass of wine. What do you think?"

Her mother grinned. "Drinking at lunch?"

"It's one glass."

"Why not? It wouldn't kill me."

Yes, and right after lunch, from the privacy of her car, Emma would put a call into their pit-bull lawyer and let her know that certain members of the Chicago Police Department were harrassing her.

THE JUDGE TOOK pity and called an early recess for the day. Zac had no issues with that and lugged his stuffed file cart out of the now-empty courtroom. Two o'clock and he hadn't eaten lunch yet. Reminding him of his crashing blood-sugar levels, a nagging ache thumped at the center of his forehead. He needed food. Fast. He'd run his cart back to the office and hit the corner deli for a bite. Then he'd study his cases for the next day.

From his right jacket pocket, his phone—the personal one—buzzed. Office phone was left pocket.

He checked it. Penny. "Hey."

"*Zachary,* I just thought you'd like to know I'm about to file a complaint against the City of Chicago."

Zac rolled his eyes. *Let the drama begin.* "Okay, Pen, I'll bite. What is your complaint?"

"It starts with the Chicago Police Department harassing Emma Sinclair. From there, I'm sure I'll come up with plenty of other misconduct violations."

Zac's headache pounded away and he closed his eyes. What the hell was Penny talking about? "What happened?"

At the elevator bank, he swung into the corner alcove and leaned against the windowsill. Afternoon sun shot rays of light against the marble floors and he centered himself in its path to soak up the heat.

"Emma and her mom had a lunch date and her mother got stopped for a broken taillight. Guess what, Zachary?"

The headache suddenly went nuclear, his skull nearly coming apart. "No broken taillight?"

"Excellent guess."

"Emma was with her?"

"They were meeting at the restaurant. Emma had just parked and saw the whole thing."

"What'd the cops say?"

Obviously reading from notes, Penny recited everything Emma had told her. He stayed quiet, listening, absorbing it all, ignoring the spine-busting grip of tension and remaining focused while the warm sun made him think of needing a vacation. "Hang on."

"What?"

"The part about the accident. They said she'd have an *accident?*"

"They implied it, yes." Paper shuffling came

from Penny's end of the line. "They said she'd better get it checked before she had an accident."

That made him boil. It was one thing to pull her over, but to imply that someone would get hurt? Epic fail. Zac stood tall, stretched his shoulders to crack his back. "You're sure that's what they said? No paraphrasing?"

"Yes. That's what Emma said. Her mother heard it."

"I'll take care of it."

"Have him hold," Penny said to someone on the other end. "Well, how about that, *The Herald* is on the other line. They're returning my call."

Damn, Penny. "You went to the press?"

"You bet your butt I did. I'm done playing. Gotta go."

The line went dead and Zac squeezed the phone hard enough to snap a knuckle. This damn case. He couldn't get a break. Witnesses, *Emma* being threatened. He didn't know how the hell to deal with that particular issue. Well, he did know, but he'd definitely lose his job if he dug his fingers into someone's throat and tore it out. Add to that his boss being mad at him for not controlling the spin and he was cooked.

And worse, he'd gotten emotionally involved with Emma. Whom he'd made love to last night, a couple of times, which he wanted to do again in the very near future.

He ran his free hand over his face. "What am I doing?"

At the window, he tilted his head to the bright sun hoping it would calm his rioting brain. *Think*. But the headache reminded him that he needed fuel. He opened his eyes and stared down at the street where a steady flow of pedestrians came and went from the building. The lunch truck was still parked at the curb.

First things first. He'd grab a sandwich from the truck, go back to his office, call Emma and get the story from her.

Then he'd kick some tail.

At least he had a short-term plan. An excellent plan. With the way this case was going, that plan would probably be blown in the next five minutes but for now it would do.

After jamming the sandwich down his throat and settling in at his desk, Zac popped three ibuprofens. Excessive, but he had King Kong tapdancing in his head. He hit Emma's number on his personal cell. Voice mail. She might already be at work. She'd mentioned it the night before.

Next he dialed Detective Leeks, that scumbag. If Leeks wanted mind games, Zac would bring it on. This guy would not threaten Emma. Not without some backlash, and Zac had enough firepower to grab the detective's attention.

Another voice mail. No one wanted to answer today. He waited for the beep. "Detective Leeks, this is ASA Zac Hennings. Have your son in my office at 9:00 a.m. tomorrow. If he doesn't show, I'll get a subpoena. Your choice, detective."

Pleased with the message, he hung up. That'd rattle some cages.

"What the hell are you doing?"

Ray stood in the hallway, hands on his hips,

his fingers drumming. *This is a problem.* Keeping his focus on his boss, he sat back, forced his shoulders down and did his best to appear casual.

"Hey, finished up early in court."

Ray stepped into the office, his face pinched and red enough that his already high blood pressure had probably spiked a couple hundred points. When he closed the door behind him, Zac tapped a foot. Ray didn't often close doors. When he did, people got a few extra holes ripped into them.

Here we go.

Ray jabbed a finger. "You're not the investigator. I talked to the SA and we assigned an investigator. You're not him. *He* will question witnesses. You want answers from the Leeks kid, you can watch from another room." Ray stopped, took a breath and dropped his hands. "I don't know what's going on with you, but you're too close to this. It's killing your judgment."

Zac stood and got eye to eye with his boss. He wouldn't yell, wouldn't wisecrack, wouldn't take an attitude. He'd just lay it out, as he always did. "What's killing my judgment is detectives and cops threatening witnesses. Emma Sinclair's mother—her mother, for God's sake—got pulled over today on a bogus stop."

"What bogus stop?"

"A busted taillight that's not busted. Emma was there and the cop told her they'd better get it fixed before her mother gets hurt."

Ray sighed.

Yeah, right there with ya, pal. "So, if I'm whacked out it's because I've had it with a small group of Chicago's finest. We need to get this Leeks kid in here and ask him if he wore a white shirt the night of Chelsea Moore's murder. Fairly simple."

Ray put his hands up. "Okay. Okay. Relax. Let's get the Leeks kid in here tomorrow. We'll have the investigator talk to him. A conversation only, nothing too hard, and see what happens. Give me a list of questions you want answered and we'll have the investigator ask."

"Ray—"

"That's the best I can do. I'm not letting you question that kid. Hell, I'm not letting you in the room. Whatever is going on with you and this detective, it's not going ballistic on my watch. Do us both a favor and back off. Got it?"

Zac didn't answer.

"I'll take that as a yes."

Ray left the office and Zac stared at the now-open doorway, pains shooting down his neck from clenched teeth. Back. Off. Handed an explosive case and the minute he uncovered something questionable, he was supposed to ease up. What they should be doing is touting a political win for the new State's Attorney, a woman who campaigned for honesty in a city plagued by corruption.

Whether Brian Sinclair was guilty or not, this case deserved a second look. Justice demanded it. Justice for Chelsea Moore, for Brian Sinclair and for Emma, who'd been fighting this battle for so long.

Maybe his emotions *were* getting in the way,

but someone had to ferret out the truth. If for no other reason than to figure out what had happened to a young woman in a dark alley, Zac wanted answers.

Either way, he wanted answers.

THIRTY MINUTES BEFORE closing time, Emma stood at the bar waiting for her customer's drink order when Zac strolled through the door. Immediately, relief flashed and spread through her. His presence did that to her, brought a sense of comfort and security to a life that had very little of either.

He spotted her, tilted his head and their gazes locked. This time, she didn't have that panicky feeling at the sight of him coming into the restaurant. After what had happened this afternoon, she'd half expected him. Penny was right about her brother. He was indeed predictable in all the ways that mattered.

But something was off about him tonight. At this late hour, he still wore his suit, minus the tie.

His shirt collar was unbuttoned and his jacket could have used a good pressing. So not Zachary. His body language wasn't right, either. Sure he'd slapped a smile on his face, but his shoulders slumped and that was one thing she'd never seen. Zac always, always, entered a room with his head high and shoulders back, his aura screaming power and control. But tonight that aura was utterly absent.

The bartender loaded drinks on her tray and she detoured in Zac's direction on her way to the table.

"Hi," she said. "I'll bet you're looking for another ferocious brownie."

"Thought I'd escort you home after your run-in with the P.D. today."

She nodded, thankful for his thoughtfulness. "I'd like that. You look sad, *Zachary.*"

That got a smile out of him. *When all else fails, do the Penny voice.*

"I'm fine. Tired."

"Everything okay?"

He glanced around the nearly empty restaurant. "Yep."

She jerked her head to the bar. "Have a seat. I'll send you a brownie."

Barely a smile out of him. Yeesh, this boy was in a world of hurt. She delivered her drinks and swung back toward the kitchen to get Zac his dessert. On the way, she noted the hostess, a perky sex kitten of a blonde, sniffing around the bar. *Hands off my man, honey.* Really, though, Emma couldn't blame the girl. Zac was definitely sniff-worthy.

Her friend Kelly marched into the kitchen behind Emma and backhanded her on the butt. "I see the hot prosecutor is back. I think Miss Emma has a boyfriend."

Emma rolled her eyes. "Emma has something. She's not sure what it is, but it definitely makes her toes curl. And that's all I'm giving you, so don't bother asking."

"Come on. Give me a little more." She squeezed

her thumb and index finger together. "Just a little."

Emma put Zac's brownie into the microwave and grinned. "He looks great naked."

"I knew it!"

The microwave dinged. She retrieved the brownie, gave it an extra scoop of ice cream and finished it with chocolate sauce, whipped cream and a cherry. He'd love this.

"Bye, Kelly."

"Oh, come on!"

"Nope." She pushed through the kitchen door, swung around the bar and slid the brownie in front of Zac. "Here you go, handsome. I made it myself." She leaned in and ran one hand over his shoulders. Locked up tight, they were. The man needed to de-stress. "It looks like you had another rough day so I gave you an extra scoop of ice cream."

"You're too good to me, Emma."

She glanced at her table then back at him.

"I don't like seeing you with a long face. It's not you."

"I'm okay."

Not for a minute did she believe it. But she had two tables to close out and she'd have to quiz him about his day when they were out of here. "I have customers. Enjoy your brownie."

Ninety minutes later, Emma parked in her minuscule driveway with Zac pulling in behind her and temporarily blocking the sidewalk. Home. Safe and sound. What a day. She'd checked on her mother a few times throughout the evening and all was quiet. No lurking cops to be found.

Zac yanked open her door, held his hand out and she grabbed it. "Thank you, sir."

"My pleasure. You gave me a brownie. Least I could do."

Once out of the car, she eased her hand away, but Zac held on, entwining his fingers with hers. Nice. They walked to the door hand in hand and Emma slowed to a crawl, wanting to prolong this feeling of being attached, of being a couple. When was the last time she'd had a casual stroll while holding hands? And was it pathetic that such a simple gesture should make her feel so desperate for the moment not to end?

Loneliness had apparently turned her into a sap because there was most likely a hateful detective watching them, taking note of the prosecutor getting friendly.

At the door, she stopped and faced Zac. "Thanks for coming home with me."

For a minute, he simply stared at her, his gaze traveling over her face until he lifted his hand and ran the back of it over her cheek. "You should have called me this afternoon. I would have helped."

She shrugged. "I wanted to."

"And what?"

"I couldn't decide if I was calling you because you're the prosecutor on my brother's case or because you're the guy I went to bed with last night. It's confusing."

He eased his hand away from her face. "Sure is."

"What happened today, Zac? Why are you sad?"

"I'm not sad. I'm frustrated. My boss thinks I've let myself get emotionally involved in this case and I can't dispute that." He puffed his cheeks up and blew out a breath. "That's tough for a trial lawyer to admit."

"I can imagine."

He leaned in, dropped a light kiss on her lips. "I worry about you. I won't apologize for that. I'm standing on this porch knowing someone could be watching and I'm not sure I care because I haven't done anything I wouldn't have done before getting involved with you. I've done my job."

Was she dreaming? Had to be. Things like this didn't happen to her. People like this, folks who fought for her, took care of her and made her believe life wasn't always a matter of handling one crisis after another. "But I don't want you risking your job for me. That's why I didn't call you today. It's not fair to you. Penny has a handle on it."

"I know she does. And, you'll find this out, but

Leeks's son is coming in tomorrow. That's what got me in the penalty box."

"Oh, Zac."

He shrugged. "I was aggravated. I know Leeks is behind those cops pulling your mom over. I figured I'd up the pressure on him. Ray heard me on the phone and reamed me out."

"I'm sorry."

"It needs to be done, Emma. It's the right thing. Someone has to question this kid without his father influencing the interview."

A girl had to love a man willing to rail against the establishment. "Obviously, I agree, but maybe you shouldn't be the one to do it."

"I'm not. Ray told me to forget it, which, at the time, aggravated me even more. Now? I agree with him. I have to be careful here. A neutral party should question that kid and I'm not neutral anymore. Not with the way I feel about you and definitely not with the way I feel about that scumbag Leeks."

Emma threw her hands up. "Okay, Mr. Prosecutor. Let's take it easy now. Don't destroy your career for me. The guilt would kill me and then I'd spend the next two years figuring out how to save *you,* too." She cracked a smile, hoping he'd grasp the sarcasm. "I'm a little tired of saving everyone. It's exhausting work."

He grabbed her around the neck and kissed her—bam—all heat and tongues and crazy, lovable passion and everything inside her burst open. *I'm crazy about him.*

Since he'd come into her life, she didn't feel so alone, so at war with the world. Being with Zac brought her peace and a sense of calm. How he did it, she wasn't sure, but he was one of those men who gave people hope.

The front door opened. "Oh!"

Emma jumped back and turned to her wide-eyed and horrified mother about to slam the door closed. Emma shoved her hand against it.

"I'm so sorry," Mom said.

"It's okay. I want you to meet someone. This is Zac. Hennings. Penny's brother."

Mom's gaze slid to Zac, then back to Emma. "He's the…"

The prosecutor. "Yes."

Zac stuck his hand out. "Mrs. Sinclair, nice to meet you. You have an amazing daughter."

"I'll agree with you there." Mom took his hand and shook it. "Nice to meet you as well. Thank you for all you've done. It has to be awkward."

Emma coughed. Then, as if sensing her misstep, Mom's eyes got big. "I mean with Penny being our lawyer. Not with…" Mom ran her palm up her forehead then held it there for a second. "I think I'll shut this door. I'm sorry, Emma. I heard you pull in and wondered where you were. I didn't know you had company."

"Zac met me at work. He didn't want me to come home alone."

Mom stared at her, a slight smile threatening before she looked at Zac. "Thank you for taking care of her."

"No problem, ma'am." He squeezed Emma's arm. "I should go. Busy day tomorrow."

The Leeks kid. Right. "I know. Thanks for bringing me home."

She wouldn't ask him to keep her posted. He was still the prosecutor and she was still the defense. *Confusing.* Besides, Penny would have her spies out and would fill her in.

Zac nodded. "Make sure you lock up. I'll call you tomorrow."

Chapter Thirteen

Ben Leeks Jr. was a bigger weasel than his father. What a conniving piece of trash this guy was. Zac watched on an oversized monitor in an office adjacent to the conference room where investigators *conversed* with Junior.

Watching this particular interview, Zac silently seethed. He wanted nothing more than to tell the kid and his lawyer to cut the nonsense and answer the flipping questions.

They'd been responding, but those responses had been in an abstract, vague way that failed to completely answer the questions. Junior's whole demeanor, the relaxed, mocking posture, the eye-rolling, all of it, stank. At least he came dressed to impress in slacks and a pressed shirt, probably his lawyer's doing. But this guy knew—*knew*—he'd be walking away a free man even if he was guilty.

His father would make sure of it.

Ray stood beside Zac, studying the screen, his arms folded. "He's not giving us anything."

"Yeah, because the lawyer isn't letting him. They've admitted he was at the club and that he left with a group. Knew that before he walked in here. We need to push harder, see if he and Chelsea argued that night."

Ray ignored the comment. No shock there. He'd made it clear he had no interest in pushing.

Zac focused on the monitor and Leeks Jr. Massive kid. Muscular and strong. Zac hit the gym four or five times a week, pumping serious iron, and yet the guy being interviewed was at least double his size. Freakishly big. *Unnatural.* "Ask him if he uses steroids."

"*What?*"

"Chelsea's friends said he was abusive. Look at

his body. He's huge. If he's taking steroids, Chelsea may have been a victim of 'roid rage."

Ray sighed.

"It happens."

"I'll have the investigator ask. Right after we get him to admit that he was wearing a white shirt that night."

Now Zac rolled his eyes. Conveniently, Junior couldn't recall what color shirt he wore the night Chelsea died.

Zac's phone buzzed. Bethenny, the office assistant. Odd. They were right down the hall. Why didn't she just come get him? "Let me take this." He pressed the button and stepped into the hallway. "Hi, Beth. What's up?"

"Sorry to disturb you. Did you have an appointment this morning?"

Zac stuck his bottom lip out, ticked through his mental calendar. Aside from court that afternoon, the Leeks interview was it. "I don't think so. Why?"

"There's a Stanley Vernon out here to see you."

Zac snapped his head up. Stanley Vernon. The State's star witness. "He didn't specifically ask for you, but he wants to see the prosecutor working the Sinclair case."

A blood rush made Zac dizzy and he shook his head. *Stanley Vernon.* "I'll be right up. Lock him in my office if you have to, but don't let him leave."

He clicked off, then stuck his head in the office where Ray continued to observe the Leeks interview. "I gotta go." Ray raised his eyebrows in that what-the-hell look Zac had gotten used to. "I know it's my case, but I've suddenly got the State's key witness wanting to see me."

"He's here?"

"In reception."

Ray jerked his chin. "Go. Don't screw up."

Thanks for the vote of confidence. "That wouldn't be my favorite option."

For a change, Ray laughed. That was progress after the tension-filled couple of days they'd had.

One thing Zac never wanted to be was the problem employee.

Forgoing the time it would take to detour to his office and grab his suit jacket, Zac hustled up the hall to the waiting area.

Beth spotted him coming around the corner and pointed to Stanley Vernon, a middle-aged man about six inches shorter than Zac. Thin with sloping shoulders, he wore a zipped-up windbreaker, jeans and the stooped look of someone carrying a heavy load.

He flipped a tan newsboy cap in his hands. Back and forth, up and down, the movement constant. Oh, yeah. This guy definitely had something on his mind.

Buzzing tension sizzled up Zac's arms. *Calm down here.* He extended his hand. "Mr. Vernon, I'm Zac Hennings. The new prosecutor on the Sinclair case."

"Hennings?"

"Yes, sir." Obviously, recognition dawned. "You

met my sister the other day. She's the defense attorney on this case."

Vernon's eyes widened. "That's…different."

No kidding. "It sure is." Zac gestured down the corridor. "Let's talk in private."

Back in his office, Zac closed the door behind them while Mr. Vernon took in the files lining the office. "These all yours?"

"Yes, sir."

"Astonishing."

"We live in a crazy world." Zac settled into his squeaking desk chair and leaned back, all calm and cool. "What can I do for you?"

Vernon stared down at the newsboy cap, flipped it a few times. "I…uh." He looked up, stared right at Zac, his eyes heavy-lidded and desperate. Fierce hammering slammed in Zac's head. Whatever the man had to say was tearing him up.

"Mr. Vernon, talk to me. I can assure you, it won't be the worst thing I've heard." Hoping to ease the strain suddenly drowning the room, he cracked a smile. "Trust me there."

More cap flipping. "Your sister and the Sin-clair girl."

"What about them?"

"They asked me questions. Got me thinking about that night."

Here it comes. "Go on."

"I was walking by the alley. It was noisy, though. The club door was open and people were in line waiting to get in. Between the talking and the music from inside I couldn't really hear any-thing."

"Okay."

"I saw someone, though, in the alley. A man. Definitely a man."

Zac would not help. Mr. Vernon had to come clean with no reminders or assistance. "I read that in your statement."

"Your sister. She asked me about the white shirt."

"Yes, sir. You testified that you saw a man in a white shirt. It's in the transcript."

He nodded. "I started thinking about that and,

you know, when the detectives questioned me? I never said anything about the white shirt."

Zac drove his feet into the floor, forcing himself to remain still, not a flinch, not a nudge. "You didn't see a white shirt?"

Slowly, with what looked like great effort, Mr. Vernon shifted his head side to side. "They told me someone else saw a white shirt."

Someone else? Who the hell was that now? Zac would have to go through Emma's files and find the other witness. After tracking down the transcripts, he'd seen that there were other witnesses called to the stand, but he didn't recall any of them mentioning a white shirt. Emma would know.

Forget keeping still. He had to move. Dispel some of the energy. He sat forward and casually leaned his elbows on the desk. "Do you remember a white shirt?"

More cap flipping. Once, twice, three times. "I don't think so."

As brutally hard as it was, Zac didn't move. He'd love to grab a notepad, but it might spook the guy. Besides, if he was about to recant—which it sounded as if he was—they'd have to write up his statement. "When you were questioned, did the detectives ask you if you remembered the white shirt?"

"Yes. They asked me and I said I wasn't sure. They said to think about it because they had another witness who said they saw someone in a white shirt. If I could agree with that, they could get the guy."

Right. Zac's guess? The other witness was bogus. Nonexistent. Detectives had probably determined that Brian Sinclair had been wearing a white shirt. Hell, Brian probably told them that himself. When Brian became the primary suspect, the P.D. wanted someone to say they saw a guy in a white shirt in that alley. Stanley Vernon was their someone.

"You agreed?"

Mr. Vernon finally set his cap on the edge of Zac's desk and pressed both hands into it before pulling back. "They seemed pretty sure that Sinclair had done it. The way they put it to me was they were just tying up loose ends. I figured since they had someone else saying they saw a white shirt, it wouldn't be just me." He stared down at his empty hands—nothing to flip—and shook his head. "I wanted to help."

For a second, Zac pitied the guy. For two years he'd been thinking that he'd helped put a killer behind bars. Now he wasn't sure and the guilt landed on him like a tanker thrown in a tornado.

"Relax, Mr. Vernon. You're doing the right thing. I appreciate your coming forward. We need to clarify what you're saying here. Okay?"

"Okay."

Zac grabbed his notepad and pen. "Let's run through it. You don't recall seeing a man wearing a white shirt?"

"I saw a man coming from the alley, but I don't know what color shirt he was wearing."

AT IT SINCE 6:00 a.m., Emma had already spent four hours of her day at the dining room table studying constitutional law. The exam was only two days away and she had a nagging sense of panic that she'd flunk. She'd never flunked a test in her life.

Never.

Maybe Zac, the lover of all things constitutional law, could quiz her. Or maybe she was just looking for an excuse to see him.

And have sex with him—lots of steamy, sweaty sex that left her loose and purring.

She ducked her head and giggled. *Bad, Emma. Bad.* Her cell phone beeped and she snatched it off the table. Zac. Their pheromones must have beelined.

"Hey, handsome. I was just thinking about you."

"What do you know about another witness identifying the white shirt?"

And hello to you, too. Forget the purring. "In reference to the white shirt, there's no other witness. Mr. Vernon was it."

"You're sure?"

Pfft. Was he serious? "Of course. I can pull the

witness files for you. I have them all sorted by time frame. If there was another witness who saw a man with a white shirt, it would be in the file with Mr. Vernon's."

"I need those files."

In the back of her brain, something snapped. A physical zap she'd never experienced against the back of her skull. "What's going on?"

"I can't say. Yet."

"You want me to turn over my files and you're not going to tell me why?"

Silence. "Do you trust me?"

Of course she did. "Completely."

"Then I need those files. You'll find out why soon."

Give him the files. She should talk to Penny first. *Give him the files.* "This is a good thing then?"

"I believe so, yes."

His answer came without hesitation. No pause, no moment to consider a response. Nothing. That had to mean something. If she truly trusted him, it meant turning over information without knowing why. Which she hadn't been inclined to do when it came to Brian.

But that snapping in the back of her head was new. Maybe a good sign. *Take a chance.*

"Give me an hour to copy the reports and get them to your office."

"Thank you."

It took Emma fifty-two minutes to call Penny, take a quick shower, copy the files and race them downtown. Penny, being Penny, went to work on her contacts to figure out what the prosecution was up to.

While Emma drove, she speculated on the sudden need for these files. It had to be something regarding the Ben Leeks interview. At a red light, she tapped the steering wheel and mulled over the options. Maybe the interview had yielded a new witness and Zac wanted to know if Emma had a statement from said witness.

From the seat beside her, the phone beeped. Still waiting for the green light, she checked the

ID and punched the speaker button. "Hi, Penny." The light changed and she made a left toward the parking garage.

"Are you there yet?"

"No. About to park."

"Park and call me. Do *not* go into that office until you talk to me."

Emma's stomach seized as she drove up to the ticket machine at the parking garage. "Is this bad?"

"No. I just don't want you driving when I tell you."

"Did we get a new trial?"

Penny huffed. "I'm not saying another word. Park and call me."

The lunatic hung up. What was that? She calls, gets Emma all wound up and then dumps her? Sheesh.

Still, her body hummed with an incessant energy, that same zapping current from before, that told her something big was about to happen. It took scouring five levels before she found an open parking space. Somehow, it seemed fitting. She'd waited all this time. Why not a few extra minutes?

She slammed the car into Park and dialed Penny. The phone beep-beeped. No signal.

"Gah! Stupid parking garage." Not a break to be had. She snatched the files and her purse and took off toward the elevator. She pressed the button. Waited and waited. The darn thing seemed to be on the second floor for a lifetime. Heck with this. She darted for the stairwell, checking her signal the whole way. Nothing.

The run down the stairs left Emma breathless, a not-so-gentle reminder that she hadn't exercised in months. Soon. With any luck, maybe soon she'd have time. Not that she'd ever had much luck, but a girl could dream.

Once on the street, three glorious bars appeared on her phone. *Thank you, signal gods.* She dialed Penny.

"What took so long?" her lawyer asked.

"Don't start. There was no signal in the garage

and then the elevator was slow. I just ran down five flights. Please tell me what's going on."

She checked traffic coming both ways and stepped off the curb.

"Mr. Vernon just recanted."

Midstride, her right knee locked and buckled. Pain shot up her thigh and she stumbled, catching the files before they fell to the ground. A horn sounded, brakes squealed and a cabbie swerved. Near miss. She gasped and clutched her folders tight while the cabbie swung his fist. Another car horn blared and she jumped back onto the curb before being flattened. Wouldn't that be the kicker? Dying just as her brother got a new trial?

"Emma?"

Recanted. That's what Penny had said. *Please, God.* She drew a bumpy breath. Why did it feel as if someone had reached into her and ripped out part of a lung?

"I'm trying not to get squashed here." On the sidewalk, Emma straightened, drew a long, slow breath and adjusted the files in her arms. "Okay. I'm good."

"We're not supposed to know this yet, but Mr. Vernon just told Zac he never saw a man in a white shirt. He definitely saw a man. No white shirt. The detectives told him another witness saw a man in a white shirt and they asked him to confirm."

Now it made sense. "Zac is looking for the witness. That's why he needs my files."

"I just talked to my dad. We don't think there's another witness. We think the cops knew Brian wore a white shirt that night so they made up this other witness to convince Mr. Vernon they had the right guy."

Please, please, please. "So Mr. Vernon's testimony will get thrown out?"

"It's enough for us to file our post-conviction petition and probably get a hearing."

"Oh, Lord." Emma hurried across the street and sprinted up the steps leading to the building where Zac's office was housed.

"Don't get crazy on me, Emma. We are still months away from a hearing. These things take time, but this is all good. Great, in fact."

In the last ten years, the Sinclairs hadn't seen a whole lot of great. Suddenly, this Hennings bunch was offering an abundance of it. "I'm heading in. I'll call you when I'm done with Zac."

"Don't let on that you know. Play dumb. Make him squirm a little."

Emma scoffed. Everything was a competition between them. They literally thrived on it. "You two make me crazy."

"I love making him wonder what I'm up to."

The line for security stretched to the lobby door and Emma almost laughed. Hadn't the last two years of her life been filled with this hurry-up-and-wait mentality? Her phone beeped again. Popular today.

Zac. "I'm stuck at security."

"Okay," he said, then silence.

"Hello?"

No answer. She held the phone in front of her. "Really now? You hung up on me? Sheesh."

Craving peace, she turned the phone off—what the point of that was, she didn't know—but it felt good. *That'll teach them.*

STILL AT HIS DESK, Zac read Mr. Vernon's statement for the thirtieth time. The man had signed it and, with his guilt slightly assuaged, had gone on his way. Mr. Vernon's statement wouldn't be enough to free Brian Sinclair from prison, and who knew if he actually belonged there, but slowly, piece by piece, the case was starting to break open.

Alex Belson, the former public defender on Brian's case, swung into the office. Interesting timing. His rumpled suit jacket and hair that stuck up on the side indicated that Alex might be having a rough day.

Zac closed the folder containing Mr. Vernon's statement. "Hey, Alex. Visiting the dark side?"

He cracked a grin, but nothing about it appeared

to come easy. "I figure it's a good reminder of why I belong elsewhere."

Zac sat back. "What's up?"

"I was in court and heard that a witness in the Sinclair case recanted."

News traveled in this building. Zac had always known that, but this was world-record speed. Being the defense attorney who took the case to trial, Alex probably wanted assurance that his butt would be covered. When it came to this convoluted mess, nobody was safe. "You heard right. Stanley Vernon."

Alex's head dropped an inch. "The guy from the alley?"

"Yeah. He came in this morning. Said the detectives implied they had a solid case against Brian Sinclair. All they needed was corroboration."

"Oh, man." Alex winced. "I should have caught that."

Probably. But given that he was the fourth PD on Brian's case, anything could have happened.

By the time Sinclair got to Alex Belson, the cops had him trussed up all nice and tidy.

"Your sister will be all over this."

"Any time now she'll have that post-conviction petition submitted."

Alex shook his head. "This case. Damn nightmare. The thing won't go away."

Not many things said in the company of trial attorneys shocked Zac anymore, but referring to the murder of a cop's daughter as *the thing* caught him short. Maybe he was wound too tight after the crazy week, but a young woman was dead, brutally murdered, and they may have incarcerated the wrong guy.

"There are issues, for sure."

Alex tapped his fingers against his leg. "Let me know if there's anything I can do."

As if Penny would let Alex Belson anywhere near this case. No. His sister would see this one to its conclusion.

Whatever that conclusion might be.

EMMA CHARGED OFF the elevator, scooted by a few milling people and raced toward the receptionist's desk. Having seen her previously, the woman waved her through. "He's waiting for you."

"Thank you."

Emma made a left, angled around a guy who looked like a lawyer and her gaze zoomed in on the man striding toward her.

Alex Belson. The useless, waste of a public defender who'd done nothing—*nothing*—for Brian. He'd barely lifted a pen. Even when Emma funneled him information from her research, he'd always come up with reasons to dismiss it.

Useless piece of garbage.

As they neared each other, his focus shifted to her, studying, remembering. He slowed his pace.

Yeah, you know me. Emma stopped in front of him, blocking his path. "I suppose you've heard the SA has assigned an investigator to my brother's case."

"I did. Good for you."

So smug. "Good for my brother. Finally."

Alex folded his arms and huffed an annoyed you-are-such-an-idiot breath. "You want to say something to me, say it."

Like a hard slap, his low, guttural tone knocked her sideways. Emma's jaw clamped tight. *Him, him, him.* Could it be? She squeezed the folders, gripped hard, her fingers nearly splitting from the pressure. *You want to die right here like Chelsea Moore?* Couldn't be. But all those times, all the evidence he'd refused to consider. She'd handed it to him. All he'd had to do was use it, which he'd never done.

Emma backed away, slowly moving around him.

"What?" he said. "You don't think I did a good job for your brother?"

"Emma?"

She turned, saw Zac striding toward her, his long legs eating up the space between them, and she wasn't sure she'd ever been so happy to see someone. The agony of her thoughts made her nauseous. What was happening? Sickness swirled and tumbled and slid and she backed up another step, needing distance. Needing *space.*

"Nice to see you again, Ms. Sinclair," Alex said from somewhere behind her.

Zac set his hand on her shoulder. Instantly, her pulse settled. His simple touch brought her mind back into focus.

"You look like hell. You okay?"

"It's him."

"Who?"

She turned back. No Alex. Gone. "Alex Belson. He's the one from the alley."

Zac dragged Emma to his office to figure out what in hell she was talking about. Something had spooked her because all color had drained from her face. Nothing left but ashy white skin.

Could this day get any more bizarre?

He shut the door behind them, took the files from her and guided her to the chair. She mumbled something and he glanced at her.

"Did Alex say something to you?"

He sat on the edge of his desk directly in front of her, their legs almost touching. The tiny lines at the corners of her mouth pinched and she brought her gaze to his. Her dark eyes locked on his so hard it could have been a punch. Emma Sinclair was one pissed-off woman.

"He's the one who attacked me in the alley."

She'd totally lost it now, but Zac would slap on his neutral prosecutor face. "Emma—"

"It's him. I recognized his voice. The tone was the same. I recognized his voice."

Complete insanity. Zac rubbed both hands over his face then looked up at the ceiling, hoping any god in the general area would send him strength.

"You think I'm crazy," Emma shot.

"I think you're under pressure."

"I know what I heard."

"We all have Chicago accents."

"Not like him you don't. The tone he used was evil. I know what I heard."

Dug in. That's what she was. And in the short time he'd known her, getting her from this line of thinking would be no easy task. Having her walking around accusing a public defender of criminal acts wouldn't do her—or Brian—a damn bit of good, either. Zac tapped his foot, twisted his lips.

"Just say it, Zac."

He held his hands up. "I've known this guy four years. He's a civil servant and you think he's a murderer?"

"I didn't say that. I think he attacked me in the alley. Why he'd do that, I don't know, but I've given up trying to figure out the things that happen in my life." She scooted to the edge of her chair and touched his knee. "I'm sure it was him."

Any time now, he could use that strength from a nearby god. Couldn't he get a break? He shook his head then jammed his palms into his eyes and pressed until his eyeballs begged for mercy. He dropped his hands, stared at Emma and wondered just what the hell they were doing. "What do you want? I can't walk into my boss's office and tell him this. I need proof. You know that. After the Leeks kid, Ray already thinks I'm in over my head. I might as well resign right now because accusing a public defender of attacking the woman I'm sleeping with won't look good in my file."

Emma gawked. "So this is about what looks good?"

"No. I want to support you. I've done nothing but support you."

"That's not true."

A rumbling in his brain alerted him to his temper firing. *Check that.* He held his breath, let it out again and cocked his head. "I've chased down every lead I could find on this case."

"You chased down those leads hoping you'd find that Brian was guilty. You didn't count on him being innocent. That's okay because you're a prosecutor and I get that. What I don't get is how you say you've supported me. You've supported me because it made sense. Suddenly, something doesn't make sense and you're backing off. I guess I'm good enough to sleep with when conditions are favorable, but now I'm a liability." She stood, waved her arms. "When did you become such a coward?"

Oh, hell no. The muscles in his neck became twisted ropes squeezed so tight that any slack was gone. Labeled a coward, he turned apoplectic. "Are you *kidding* me? You think anyone else around here would take on this mess?"

The second—make that millisecond—the words left his mouth, he regretted them. *Damn temper.* Words like that could slice a woman in two.

"Now I'm a mess? My brother being falsely convicted is a mess? A *mess?*"

"That's not what I meant!"

She held her hands in a stop motion and jerked them at him. Hauling her shoulders back, she closed her eyes and curled her fingers. Within seconds, she opened her eyes again, her body not as stiff and outraged. "Forget it. This is getting us nowhere and it makes us both look bad. I know how that upsets you. But hey—" her voice was low, as if a thousand soldiers had pummeled it

"—I guess it's time for you to learn that life isn't always fair. Believe me."

She swung away from him and cruised to the door. No drama, no stomping feet, no carrying on.

"Emma!"

She opened the door and held it so it wouldn't bump the wall.

Without glancing back, she said, "I think we're done here. Thanks so much for your time."

EMMA RACED FROM the elevator, blew by slower people standing in the lobby and focused on the exit, the one leading to fresh air. She'd been so stupid to think she could depend on anyone from the State's Attorney's Office to help them.

And she'd slept with him. Let him invade her not-so-iron heart. Heartbreak, at this point, was the last thing she needed. Not when life seemed to be on an upswing. Well, an upswing graded on the curve of Emma's crappy luck.

Now she had to deal with this attachment to Zac

because as furious as she was with him right now, a slow-growing ache had formed in her chest— one she didn't want to feel. She knew what it was. This was how it started with her. She'd ignore the ache, work around it, justify it, whatever.

Then one morning she'd wake up paralyzed, unable to move or breathe or function and her world would be empty and suffocating and she'd want to pound on something until all that hurt and anger went away.

Broken hearts totally stank and something told her Zac Hennings had just made the first crack in hers.

Chapter Fourteen

Deciding he could stand some fresh air, Zac took an early lunch and called his father. At certain times in his life, regardless of his father's current status as the opposition, Zac gave in to the idea that he still needed his dad's counsel.

In a matter of days, he'd gone from the office pit bull to a guy his boss couldn't trust. All because of a woman he'd slept with.

Epic fail.

Zac stepped into the glass-walled lobby of his father's office building and waved to the guard. Hennings and Solomon didn't have the entire building. They had three floors, though, and the guards had seen Zac often enough to know him.

He signed in at the desk and made his way to the tenth floor. The receptionist juggled multiple ringing lines, but pointed him in the direction of his father's office, which worked for him, since he was in no mood for small talk. He'd even taken the long way to his father's office in a pansy attempt to avoid Penny.

When Zac stepped into the office, his father was holding the phone to his ear and rocking back and forth in his desk chair. He waved him in.

"My son is here. I'll call you back."

That fast, his father had rearranged his priorities, putting Zac at the top. No matter how old they got, his father always made time for his children. A good lesson to remember. And suddenly Zac had a vision of Emma chasing after a bunch of kids. His kids.

Where's this going now? He shook it off. No time for those fantasies. Plus, she currently wasn't speaking to him, much less wanting to have his babies.

As usual, his father shook his hand then brought

him in for a shug—the combo shoulder pat and hug.

"Nice seeing you, son."

"You, too, Dad."

His father stepped back, ran a hand down his custom-made shirt. "Have a seat."

"Mind if I close the door?"

"With a lunch-hour visit, I assumed this would be a closed-door session."

Just as Zac grabbed the door, Penny stormed by then skidded to a halt. Too slow for his sister, she set her hand on the door and squeezed into the office.

Her blue eyes drilled him. "What's this about?"

"I'm here for Dad."

Penny blew that off. "Emma told me about Alex Belson."

"I'm not discussing this with you."

"What about Alex Belson?" Dad wanted to know.

Penny kept her focus on Zac. "It's worth looking into. She said you wouldn't even consider it."

His sister was such a pain in the ass. "This might shock you, but I can't charge a PD without proof."

"What about Alex?" Dad asked again.

But Zac was rendered mute by Penny's accusing glare. She had something brewing in that crazy brain of hers and it couldn't be good. Not with the way she focused on him, her gaze sliding over his face pondering, considering.

"Hey," Dad said in that slow, controlled voice that let them know his patience was wearing thin. "Someone answer me."

Zac faced him. At least until Penny lunged and landed a not-so-gentle punch on his right arm that sent a stab of pain clear to the bone. For a small woman, she had some fire. "Ow. What's that for?"

"You slept with our client! I can see it on your face, Zachary. Guilt. You *pig*."

"What the…?" Zac slid a desperate, sideways glance at their father. *Please help me.*

"Penny," Dad said. "Out. Now."

But Penny remained in her spot, her lips pinched and—if he knew his sister—holding back a whole lot of mean. "I knew you had a thing for her. I *can't* believe you."

Again, she whacked him on the arm. Now he'd had it. He didn't blame her for being mad, but he'd had enough of the drama-girl routine. "Hit me again and I'll move you out of here myself."

Dad stood. "Penny, *out*."

"Dad!"

Dad pointed to the door. "Out."

Suddenly, Penny was twelve again, throwing a fit because the boys got to play outside after dark.

Her perfect little nose wrinkled and she waved her fist at him. "Pig!"

Needing a minute, Zac jammed his palms into his eye sockets. This was so seriously messed up. He dropped his hands. "She's insane. I mean, is there any chance we're not from the same gene pool? Maybe I'm adopted and didn't know it?"

His father grinned. "Unless your mother is keeping a secret, I'm confident you're both mine." He gestured to the chair. "Tell me what's on your mind."

He dropped into the plush leather guest chair so unlike the crummy metal ones in his office. Everything about this office—the rich woods, the neat shelves stocked with law books, the orderly appearance of the desk—all of it screamed control and organization. "I think I screwed up."

"If you had sex with our client, I'd say you're right."

"Emma." *Ah, cripes.* Admitting this violation wouldn't be easy and Zac's stomach heaved. "I, uh…"

His father sat forward and folded his hands on the desk. "Your sister's assessment is correct?"

Thank you. "Yeah, but it's not ugly. Not like she made it sound. Emma is amazing and smart and dedicated. Who wouldn't want her?"

Dad held his hands up. "You're both unattached, responsible people. Things happen. But you're the prosecutor. An intimate relationship subjects your case to scrutiny. You know that."

"Exactly."

"You should have kept your hands off her until this case was over." He smacked a hand on the desk. "That didn't happen. So let's figure it out. You had a fight with Emma over Alex Belson?"

Right. Alex. "You know about Emma getting attacked in the alley."

"Yes."

"Alex came by my office this morning. He'd heard that Stanley Vernon recanted."

No reaction to this news. His father remained quiet. "Dad, I know you know. You've got spies everywhere."

Dad rolled his bottom lip out. "We'd heard something."

"Alex was curious about Vernon's statement. I didn't think much of it. I know I'd be curious if a witness on a case I'd worked recanted. Emma ran into him when he left my office. She looked upset and I asked her what happened." Zac threw his hands up. "She tells me she thinks *Alex* attacked her in the alley."

If trial lawyers got Oscars, Zac's father would have a few—more than a few. When it came to an unruffled performance, he was a master. "You think she's imagining it?"

"No."

"Then what's the problem?"

"I'm not objective anymore. I froze. Part of me wanted to get nuts and protect her. She does everything herself. I hate that. But Ray is all over me on this. I was supposed to make it go away."

"And you didn't."

"I wanted to. I wanted Brian Sinclair to be guilty. I *wanted* to tell Chelsea Moore's family that we got it right the first time. Instead, I told my boss to assign an independent investigator because the case is seriously flawed."

His father sat back and took it all in. If a lecture was forthcoming, Zac knew he deserved it. His father's lectures were legendary. A person could turn to stone once Dad got rolling. Now, though, he was probably muted by his son's failures. Finally, he sat forward, leaning in, engaging. "What can I do?"

No lecture. *Got lucky.* Zac dragged his fingers through his hair, then tugged. Damn, his head hurt. How did he start feeling so old and exhausted? This case and the emotional warfare, that's how. "I don't know. I had to blow off steam."

"I see that." Dad let out the three-thousand-pound sigh. Zac hated that sigh. "You need to talk to Emma. Tell her you care. My guess is she doesn't know you're invested. She thinks you're willing to sacrifice her for your career."

Point there.

"Are you?"

Zac glanced up. Staring into his father's eyes, he knew the answer. Clear as day. "No."

"Kid, you're in a jackpot here."

"Thanks, Pop."

"What you need to do is make her understand that you care, but back away. You have to. She knows as well as you do that this relationship is dangerous."

"I know."

"Then you put this Belson thing aside. I'll get one of my investigators on it. See if there's something there. This case has so many twists and turns, anything is possible." He drove his index finger into the desktop. "You stay away from Emma until this is over. You hear?"

"I know."

"But you did it anyway."

"Dad—"

"No excuses. Impropriety could destroy your career and keep this kid in prison when he doesn't belong there."

Guilt, hot and slick, shot up Zac's neck. His father was right. Distance from Emma was the smart move. He'd talk to her. Explain his position. Convince her it was the right thing for both of them. Then he'd walk away.

Temporarily.

He hoped.

After the you're-my-son-but-you-screwed-up talk, Zac detoured to Penny's office. He pushed the partially open door in. His sister sat behind her massive desk, doing something on her computer. She spotted him and shot him the death glare again.

She folded her arms. "Zachary."

"Where's Emma?"

"Dream on. You've done enough for one day." She sat forward and poked a finger at him. "You upset my client. For this, I will shred you in court. You'll *beg* me to stop."

His baby sister, warrior queen. "Spare me. I care about her." She opened her mouth, but he waved. "Forget it. Not discussing it. I have to talk to your client. Where was she when you spoke to her?"

Penny spun back to her computer and Zac stared up at the ceiling. *It'll be a miracle if I don't kill her.* He closed his eyes, took a few breaths and thought about an ice cold beer on a beach, in a hammock maybe. Breaking ocean waves... Sleep.

A minute later, after somehow finding the patience not to strangle his sister, he glanced back at her. "Great. Thanks for your help."

On his way out the door Penny said, "She's on her way home."

He turned back. "Thank you."

"You're killing me, Zachary."

"If it makes you feel any better, *I'm* killing me. This thing with Emma, it's not..." He stopped. He didn't know what it was. "I never expected to care."

Penny shifted front and dropped her hands on her desk, her gaze straight-on. "She's been through a lot. I've gotten to know her and she seems happy. As happy as someone in her position can be. She's coming out of the dark."

"I know."

"Then don't break her heart or I'll have to stab you."

She'd do it, too. He twisted his lips, made a show of rolling his eyes, but really, he wanted to hug her. She was a drama aficionado, but he loved her. "I'll fix it."

It took thirty-five minutes—long past Zac's lunch hour—to get through downtown traffic and reach Emma's Parkland neighborhood. On the way, he called Diane, his co-counsel on the murder case currently in jury selection, and asked her to handle the afternoon session. She had a better grasp of the case anyway and would be fine on her own.

He made the left leading to Emma's street and found it blocked by fire engines and patrol cars. Black, billowing smoke rose into the air from three doors down.

Sweat peppered his upper lip and he swiped at it. "What's this now?"

He parked at the curb and got out. A cop standing at the barricade held his hand up.

Zac flashed his credentials. The cop studied the gold-toned badge and glanced back at Zac who jerked his chin toward the emergency vehicles. "What's happening?"

"House fire."

His stomach pinched. *Couldn't be.* "You know the address?"

"225. White, two-story."

Bam—he might as well have been sucker punched. The hot dog he'd grabbed on the way over flipped like a gymnast in his gut. His vision swam for a minute. *Focus.*

"You okay?" the cop asked.

In his mind, he pictured Emma trapped in a burning home, overcome by smoke, falling over... *Stop.*

"Is anyone hurt? I was headed there. I'm a... friend of the family. How bad is it?"

"No one home. They're still knocking down the fire."

A car pulled up behind Zac, the rattle of its engine sounding all too familiar. For a moment, he couldn't move, the relief immobilizing. He massaged his forehead, his mind already moving to the next task.

He inched around. "This is the owner's daughter. She lives there."

"She can't go in."

"I know. I'll take care of it."

EMMA TURNED HER car off and stared at the thick, black smoke coming from the center of her block.

For a moment, she sat nestled in her seat belt, valiantly attempting to ignore her body's warning signals. The throbbing temples, the fierce pain shooting across her forehead and the flashes of white blinding her. She pushed the car door open and headed for the barricade where an officer stood with—Zac.

Why was he here?

She picked up her pace, her gaze cemented to the swirling red lights in the middle of the block. Zac's face—*oh no*—his face held the drawn look of a man about to be strapped into the electric chair.

She kept moving, though, staying focused on

the middle of the block that, from the look of Zac, couldn't be anything she wanted to see.

Four feet from him, she pointed. "Is that my house?"

Surprisingly, the words came fast and direct. No shaking voice. No obvious panic. If they only knew.

"Emma—"

She pushed by him. "What's on fire?"

The officer slid in front of her. "Sorry, ma'am."

"Is that my house?" Zac grabbed her arm, but she jerked it free. "Tell me."

"Yes."

Blood roared. Just a screaming, pounding, eviscerating surge shredding her body. "Where's my mother?"

Zac eyed the cop.

"No one inside," he said.

For once, she gave in, let the momentum take her and she stepped back, forcing herself to stay upright. Her mother was safe. Zac grabbed her elbow. Slowly, her body in low gear, churning through the thick mud of information, she turned to him.

"Emma? Talk to me."

Her mother was safe. That should have been enough. As relieved as she was, Brian's ticket to freedom sat in boxes—*three high, six across*—in the basement. They'd barely put a dent in copying them. All her work, all her hopes, all her mother's dreams could be burning.

She had to get there. Had to see what was left. Couldn't stand here and wait. God, she was so tired of waiting. She sucked air through her nose, stared up at the thick black smoke and the overwhelming urge to tear the living hell out of something consumed her. Raw energy sliced down her arms into her fingers. She shook her hands, flexing and unflexing.

"Emma?"

The sound of Zac's voice. The man who'd lost faith in her and thought she was crazy only added to the agony and she backed up. Three steps. Then another for the extra room. That black smoke continued to torment her. *I need to see it.*

The cop's radio crackled and he unclipped it from his shoulder, spoke into it and turned his back to her.

Run.

She burst into a sprint, barreling around the edge of the barricade.

"Emma!" Zac hollered.

She heard the cop yell, but didn't dare slow down. She'd be there in seconds.

All at once, the house, the trucks, the firefighters, the billowing smoke came into view and she halted in the middle of the street. Ugly, flashing flames shot from the first-floor windows while firefighters yelled commands and directed thousands of gallons of pressurized water into the inferno. Fear spiked and she held her breath, willed herself to look at the basement window next to the porch.

Maybe it's not the basement.

Orange-tipped flames, almost beautiful in their

slashes of color, flicked from the window and Emma knew.

An insane howling roared up her throat, clawing its way out and her legs wilted. Her head whirled and she held her arms wide looking for anything solid to cling to.

"Emma!" Zac yelled.

A chunk at a time, the emotional assault wrecked her and her body gave out. She dropped to the ground in a wailing lump.

All the evidence gone. The files, the photos, the time lines—everything. Gone.

Her chest tore open, a good solid rip that left her exposed and vulnerable. And still she screamed. *Crack.* She glanced up as the porch overhang toppled.

Can't breathe.

Out of oxygen, she finally stopped screaming. She sucked in huge gulps of air. *Please, more air.* On all fours, she stared down at the grass and tears dropped from her cheeks to the backs of her hands.

Zac kneeled in front of her and she sat back. He cupped her cheeks in his hands. His mouth moved, but she heard nothing.

Chaos. Everywhere. *Make it stop.*

She jerked her head from his hands. The one who thought she was crazy.

Again, he grabbed her and held on. "Emma!"

Why is he here? The sound of his voice, commanding but gentle, broke through and she focused on steadying breaths. All surrounding movement drifted away. The roaring dulled and the agony in her chest eased. Sanity returning. "Zac?"

"You're okay, honey. You're okay." He let go, wrapped his arms around her and held tight. "I've got you."

He had her. He sure did. In a matter of hours he'd managed to devastate her then showed up to help. Would her life ever get uncomplicated?

"Why are you here? Did you know?"

He inched back. "No. I came to talk to you about this morning."

Oh, God. She wasn't ready for that. Not with this simmering anger, this *grief* over allowing herself to fall for a man she'd known would sacrifice her to get a win.

"All my files. They're gone."

"We don't know that yet."

A firefighter yelled and Emma averted her eyes, not wanting to see the charred remnants of their home. *Mom.* "I have to find my mother. I can't let her come home to this."

"Where is she?"

"I think she went shopping." She slapped her hands over her face then dragged them down. "This will kill her."

Zac stood, held his hand to Emma. "Start calling. I'll get with someone from the fire department, see what's what." He motioned to the house. "Maybe it'll only be the first floor."

And the basement. Where all the files relating to Brian's case, a recently very active case, were stored.

"I think someone torched my house. *Someone* wanted to destroy my files."

Someone who knew she had the only extensive evidence collection.

"Stop. Let me talk to the chief."

Emma snatched her phone from her jacket pocket. She had to find her mother. "That's fine, but this was no coincidence, Zac. And you know it."

ZAC'S THOUGHTS ZINGED like bullets at a firing range. As much as he wanted to believe that Emma's house going up in flames could be an accident, his mind wouldn't wrap around it. The house was old, at least seventy-five years old, so, yeah, it was possible something shorted and—zap—the house is flambé.

He grunted and dragged his hands over his head. Emma and her mom sat on the back step of the ambulance while Emma did what she could to console her mother. Not that it appeared to be working because Mrs. Sinclair wore the bombed-out look of a woman caving in.

Out of the corner of his eye, a flash of pink came into view. Popsicle Penny on a direct course to Emma and Mrs. Sinclair. Zac hustled over and intercepted his sister.

"Hey," she said. "How are they?"

He shrugged. "How should they be? We need to find them a place to stay."

"I did it already."

Probably a hotel. "Something better than a hotel. A condo or a rental house. Homey."

"Zac, I'm on it. One of our clients is out of the country for a year. His apartment is empty. Dad called him and he said they can stay there. It's seven thousand square feet and has a view of Navy Pier. I think they'll be comfortable."

I'll say.

"Penny?" Emma called.

Penny waved. "Let me talk to them, and you and I need to huddle. Something is seriously whacky here."

He stood off to the side, giving her privacy with her clients. When she reached them, Penny squatted to eye level and touched Mrs. Sinclair's knee. His sister was a lunatic, but she had a way of connecting with people on an emotional level. A gift she could turn on and off at will.

Another gene pool issue because Zac hadn't inherited that gift.

He slid his phone from his pocket, scrolled his contacts until he found Tom Carson, the investigator assigned to the Sinclair case.

"Carson," the man barked. He would never be congenial but he got his job done.

"Hey, Tom. Zac Hennings."

"What you got?"

"Do me a favor. See if you can find out where Ben Leeks was this afternoon."

"Junior or Senior and why?"

Zac glanced back at the smoldering house, then to Emma who still sat on the back of the ambulance talking to Penny. She didn't deserve this.

"Both. The Sinclairs' home had a fire."

"Torched?"

"Not sure. If it wasn't, it's an interesting co-incidence. From the looks of the place, all of Emma's files are gone."

"Ah, that's rough. I'll get into it."

"Thanks. Where are we with Junior?"

"It looks like his alibi checks out. I talked to a bunch of his friends, plus some of Chelsea's. In a twisted way, I think he loved her. This kid's a numbskull, but murder? I'm not getting that."

Not exactly a surprise to Zac. "And the white shirt?"

"I can't find another witness who saw a guy in white. My take? The detectives knew Sinclair was wearing a white shirt and fed it to Stanley Vernon."

"To sum things up, Leeks is clean, the white shirt is out and Vernon has recanted."

Welcome to the afternoon showing of his case falling apart.

"You got it, hoss. Anything else?"

Alex. Zac rolled his lips in—*can't go there.* No

proof. If he put an investigator on it, someone, somewhere in a position higher than Zac's would find out and his butt would be in trouble deep. Deeper than he already was.

"You there?"

A firefighter trudged by, dragging a giant iron tool. No idea what that was for, but the sight of it brought Zac to the injustice done here today. "One more thing: I'd appreciate your keeping it quiet, but see where Alex Belson was today. He's a Cook County public defender."

Tom let out a low whistle.

"Exactly. I'm way out on this. It's probably nothing."

"I'll look into it."

"Thanks. I need one more thing."

"What's that?"

"His address."

Chapter Fifteen

Emma watched Zac shove his phone back in his jacket pocket and glance at the remnants of her mother's home. Of *her* home.

The fire department's battalion chief had said the blaze went no higher than the first floor but water damage was extensive. The house would no doubt need to be gutted. All that remained in the basement was the charred wreckage of Penny's copy machine. Fascinating. Months and months of Emma's sweat gone and, with it, probably Brian's chance at freedom. She'd never give up, though.

Never.

She'd simply start again.

If they found that this was an act of arson, she'd hunt down the person responsible. She'd had enough resistance in her life to know how to fight back. Every day she'd work toward making her mother's life whole again, even if it meant giving up her own dreams.

"Okay," Penny said. "Let's call your insurance company. They'll get the house boarded up."

"I'll call," Mom said.

Before she could check herself, Emma swung her head sideways, her shock obvious to anyone within ten feet.

"Don't look so surprised," Mom snapped. "It's still my house."

Nice, Emma. Way to make your mother feel useless. "I know. I'm sorry. I just thought...I can do it."

"I know what you thought and I don't blame you. Makes me realize how much I've placed on your shoulders. I'll deal with the insurance company. If I need help, I'll ask."

Thank you. Emma wrapped her arm around her mother's shoulder and squeezed. "That's awesome, Mom. I love you. I promise we'll get this fixed. All of it."

Penny rose from her squatted position and surveyed the mess. "I'll talk to the chief and see if you'll be able to get in there. Until they're done investigating, I doubt it, but we'll see. Then I'll take you to your fancy new apartment. Sound good?"

"Yes," Mom said, her voice steady. Determined. "Sounds fine."

Maybe my mother is back.

Emma stood, wrapped Penny in a hug. "Thank you."

"You're welcome. I hate this for you."

Looking over Penny's shoulder, Emma spotted Zac talking with one of the firefighters. She still didn't truly understand why he was here, but at the moment, despite the emotional bloodbath unleashed on her, she should at least talk to him. "I need to speak to your brother."

Penny backed away and eyeballed her. "I could slap the two of you. I told you not to sleep with him."

A blast of horror snaked up Emma's throat.

How embarrassing that Penny had figured out they'd, as Brian would say, done the nasty. Emma snorted. Even from prison, her brother made her laugh.

Exhaustion. It had to be exhaustion.

Penny jerked her head. "Talk to him. I don't want to hear about it. Not one thing."

"Yes, ma'am."

She wandered over to Zac, slowing as she got closer. Suddenly, she wasn't sure her presence would be welcome. Not after her little psychomeltdown in the street. His gaze shifted from the firefighter for a second and—*oh, what a guy*—he held his hand to her.

All she had to do was take it. Simple gesture. Sure they had issues to deal with, but if she chose to reject and embarrass him by not accepting the comfort he offered, they were as good as done. Like any man, Zac had his pride and she couldn't disrespect him. Not after all he'd done for them. Still, she was far from ready to pick up where they were before their fight.

If she couldn't trust him to support her, there was no point in allowing the relationship to continue. And he'd made it clear that his job was his priority.

The firefighter shifted to the side and nodded. Zac's hand still hung in midair. *Grab it*. No. *Don't embarrass him*.

She reached for his hand and held it. No squeeze, no caressing fingers, no indication of anything. Brutal compromise. The loose hold he had on her indicated his understanding.

Yeah, we've got some work to do.

"This is Emma Sinclair."

"Sorry about this," the firefighter said. "We'll be out of here soon."

The man left and Zac faced her, his fingers still linked with hers, barely hanging on.

"Penny told you about the apartment?"

Emma looked into his spectacular blue eyes, which always settled her. "Yes. She's amazing."

"I wouldn't go that far."

He smiled, though, and a piece of Emma's broken heart sheared off. Truth was she didn't know how to love the man prosecuting her brother's case. "I'm sorry we had a fight," she said.

"Me, too. I didn't like that. At all."

"I don't know how to do this, Zac."

"Me, neither."

"Penny was right. We have no business being in a personal relationship right now." She waved toward the house. "And after this…all my evidence…" Her voice hitched and she breathed in. *You can do this.* "I have no idea what will happen with Brian's case."

"There are some copies left."

"Not enough, Zac."

"I told Tom Carson to see where the Leeks kid was this afternoon. And Alex Belson."

After her house almost burned to the ground, he finally believed her. Still, he'd gotten there. Not that anything could change between them. "Thank you. I know that couldn't have been easy for you, but thank you."

"I want to support you, Emma. This thing is

moving fast. I need a second to catch up. Form a plan. You're good at shifting on the fly. I need to process. Collect proof to back up my gut reactions."

"I shouldn't have hit you with the Alex thing and expected you to do something right then. I didn't think it through, but that's me. That's how I operate and I can't change that. If you weren't the prosecutor on our case, it wouldn't be an issue. I can't get around that. And, if Brian's petition is denied, he'll stay in prison. You'll be the one who kept him there. How would a relationship between us survive that?"

"Emma—"

She stepped back. "I know myself. At some point, I'll look at you and wonder if you could have done more. It wouldn't be fair, but I'd do it."

He nodded. Maybe he understood. God knew she didn't. "I'm sorry, Zac. It's over."

LONG AFTER PENNY installed Emma and her mother in their temporary digs, Zac stood on the sidewalk waiting for the arson investigator to come outside. Maybe he could give Zac the 411 on whether his findings were heading in the direction of arson.

Plus, Zac was in no hurry to be anywhere in particular. Not after Emma gave him the drop-kick. All he'd wanted was for them to lie low until Brian's case got settled. Apparently, she had a different idea.

He propped an arm on a low tree branch and tapped his fingers against it. He couldn't think too hard about Emma. Wallowing in misery wasn't his style, but this feeling of each breath being trapped inside a crushed torso did nothing for his state of mind.

Better to focus on the Sinclair home and the implications it might have. In his gut, Zac had no doubt that someone had intentionally done this. No doubt whatsoever. Call it intuition or plain common sense, but he knew.

His phone rang. Ray. This would be a problem, considering that Zac was supposed to be in court and had asked his co-prosecutor on the trial to cover for him.

He clicked the answer button before it went to voice mail. "Hey, Ray."

"Where the hell are you?" his boss thundered.

"I'm at the Sinclair place. Someone torched it."

"Did you forget we're in the middle of jury selection?"

"I talked to Diane. It was a short day today. I figured she could handle it while I waited on the arson investigator."

"He'll send you a report."

"He's finishing up. Maybe he'll give me something."

"I don't know what you're doing. You're killing your career."

Ah, damn. *There's always the private sector.* He'd hate that, though. He thrived on being a trial lawyer and somehow he didn't see himself making the leap from prosecution to defense. Plenty of attorneys did, but he wasn't sure it was for him. Civil law might be an option. Another thing he couldn't think about now. "You told me to figure it out. Not my fault it isn't the direction you wanted."

"I'm about to pull you from this case."

Not a chance. But he'd stay calm. No yelling. "I'm making progress here. However this plays out, we can spin it so it works for Helen Jergins. If Sinclair is guilty, we'll prove it once and for all. If he's innocent, she's freed a wrongfully convicted man. Either way, it's good."

"You'd better hope it's good or you'll have bigger problems than just being pulled off this case."

A slam came from the other end. *Ooosh.*

Zac pulled the phone from his ear. Stared at it a minute. His boss had just threatened his job. Seriously? *Seriously?*

If doing the right thing got him this garbage, why bother? He'd never considered himself an idealist when it came to politics and he knew there were times political maneuvering dictated the outcome of a case, but he'd never been pushed face-first into it.

Emma had been fighting this wall of opposition for too long. Day after day of roadblocks. Of people telling her *no* and expecting her to accept it. Hell, he'd been one of them.

For him, it had been a week and he'd already hit overload. No wonder she'd flipped over his need for proof about Alex.

The arson investigator, Dick Jones, walked out of the house. Zac had introduced himself earlier and had told the man he'd be waiting.

"I can't give you anything official," the inspector said.

"I know. This is off the record, so to speak. Goes nowhere outside of this conversation."

Dick nodded. "Heavy charring in the basement and on the first floor. Also charring and smoke stain on the ceiling toward the back."

"Origin?"

"Looks like the basement floor. The stairs leading to the first floor were burned through. Based on the condition of the floor and the pattern of the burn, I'd say it's arson."

Emma was right. "You'll be finished when?"

"Tomorrow. I'll write up my report as soon as we wrap up here."

Zac glanced up at the house. "Can anything be salvaged?"

"Maybe some clothes. Stuff from the second floor, but it all needs cleaning. A real mess."

This guy had no idea. "Thanks. I appreciate the info."

"No problem. Don't jump the gun on me."

Zac shook his head. "No. We're good." His phone rang and he checked it. Tom Carson. "I gotta take this. Thanks again."

He headed to his car at the end of the block. Almost four o'clock and he was still here. No wonder Ray was pissed.

"Hey, Tom."

"Leeks Senior was in court testifying this afternoon. The kid was at work today. Apparently he's a personal trainer and had clients until two."

Eh, there went that idea. Even if Junior didn't

set the fire, he could still be involved. And his father couldn't be ruled out, either.

"Where this gets interesting," Tom said, "is Alex Belson."

Zac stopped walking and a car flew by him, the driver honking the horn and nearly giving Zac an explosive bowel movement. "Take it easy!"

People.

"You okay?" Tom asked.

"Yeah. Alex Belson?"

"He left court around eleven."

Which was right around the time he showed up at Zac's office. "He came to see me."

"Oh." Tom paused. Probably making a note. "How long was he with you?"

"Less than ten minutes. He walked out of my office then ran into Emma Sinclair. Couldn't have been more than fifteen minutes total he was in our office. Where did he go after that?"

"That's what's interesting. He called his office, probably when he left you and told them he was on lunch."

"Return time?"

"One-thirty."

Come again? Zac stood frozen. A two-and-a-half hour lunch.

"And before you ask, yes, I double-checked it. I have two people who confirmed it. Plus, he swiped his key card when he entered the office. The guard verified it."

He reached his car and leaned against the hood. "Any idea where he went to lunch?"

"None."

"Okay. How about his address?"

"I've got it."

Jumping into the car, Zac grabbed his notepad from the glove compartment. "Go."

"If I give this to you, are you gonna do anything stupid?"

"No."

"Zac?"

"Tom, I promise you. Nothing stupid. I'll have my sister put an investigator on him. See if he's up to anything. I don't want the SA's office behind it. That's all."

And I want to make sure he doesn't go near Emma. Zac didn't want to believe this guy was capable of attacking Emma or setting this fire, but he wouldn't take a chance. He shook his head, hoping some form of understanding over this screwed-up scenario would flash into his mind.

No luck. Tom rattled off the address.

"Do I want to ask what Brian Sinclair's former public defender might have to do with the fire at the Sinclairs'?"

Zac dropped the notepad and sat back in his seat. "I wish I knew, Tom. I wish I knew."

Chapter Sixteen

Emma walked out of the restaurant's kitchen, untied her apron and shoved it into her tote bag. Her feet did the normal protest and she eyed one of the barstools. If she sat down, though, she wouldn't get up. She'd crash right there and let the stress of the day seep from her body. She'd known plenty of exhaustion in her life, but this heaviness, which slowed her steps and made her dream of sleeping for a month, had kicked her to another level of tired.

Days didn't get any longer than the one she'd just had. Part of her had considered calling off work, but sitting around a strange apartment—no matter how stunning it was—thinking about her decimated home and her broken heart, courtesy of Zachary Hennings, wouldn't fix her problems. Plus, they'd need extra money for whatever deductibles the insurance company would hit them with.

The hostess locked the front door while they closed up. No Zac tonight. That's what happened when a relationship ended. All those comforting moments, like him showing up to see her home, went away and left that monstrous black sinkhole inside waiting for her to slide in and get smothered.

Not going to happen.

She'd long ago given up on happily ever after. The way her life went, if she found someone to share a happily-ever-after life with, they'd wind up getting run over by a bus. At least they'd die together. For some reason, she found that thought vaguely amusing and quietly laughed.

So morbid, Emma. And so unlike her. As much as people teased her about her willingness to persevere, she'd take it over this nonsense any day.

What good would sitting here boo-hooing do? She needed rest and a good dose of Warrior Emma. At least that Emma knew how to move ahead.

"No guy tonight?" the hostess asked.

"No," Emma said, the word oozing from her mouth. "Emilio said he'd walk me to my car. He's finishing up in the kitchen."

Hoping to avoid further questions from the nosy hostess, Emma turned, faced the front window and—wham—her heart exploded, one giant blast of energy that made her arms tingle. On the other side of the glass, in the misty, freezing rain, Zac stood bundled in a coat and ski hat.

He's here. Emma leaped off the stool, buttoned her jacket and rushed to the door while the hostess flipped the lock.

"I thought you were waiting for Emilio."

"Um, no. Tell him thanks, though. Zac is here."

She scooted out before the litany of busybody questions came. Moist air smacked her cheeks and cars whooshed by, their tires kicking up water from the rainy evening. Emma pulled her hood up. "Hi."

"Hi back."

"You came."

A half smile quirked his lips. "Just because you dumped me doesn't mean I can't make sure you get home."

She dumped him. For good reason. At least she thought. *What am I doing?*

Something in her throat squeezed and her eyes throbbed. *No tears.* She swallowed once, warring with herself to keep it together. "I'm so confused and miserable. I don't know what to do."

He skimmed his finger over the curve of her cheek to her jaw and that light touch, so gentle and comforting, sent her into another battle with self-doubt. How could she let him go?

"Me, too," he said. "But it's been a lousy day and talking about it now won't help."

"You're always so logical."

"It's what I do." He jerked his chin toward the street. "Where are you parked?"

"Two blocks down. I got to work late and had to park in the garage."

"Let's get you there then. The roads are horrible. Freezing rain iced everything over. Drive slow tonight."

They walked in silence, the swish of tires against pavement providing a diversion to the destruction lying heavy between them. For once, they had nothing to say. How incredibly sad for both of them.

In the near distance, the parking garage loomed and Emma slowed. Pathetic? Yes. But she didn't want this time with him to end. If Brian didn't win a reversal, there'd be no future with Zac and it would be best if she just let him go now. Save herself the pain later. How sad that her life had become a study in saving herself pain.

At the corner, they waited for the walk sign to flash. A few cars idled at the red light, but all in all, a quiet night. The light changed and Zac stepped off the curb. On the cross street, a driver gunned the gas to make a left, spotted Zac in the street and slammed on his brakes. The car slid as if greased.

No.

Tires squealed from the opposite direction and Emma grabbed Zac's coat, hauling him backward as a speeding car barreled into the car making the left. An enormous crash of metal and shattering glass erupted and then, in seconds there was nothing but silence. Harsh, ugly silence.

Only feet in front of them was the wreckage of a destroyed vehicle, the windshield of the speeding car had blown out and a passenger lay draped across the dash into the open space where glass had been. No seat belt. Whether the person was male or female, Emma couldn't tell. Too much blood. Awful, soaking amounts of blood.

Zac tore into the fray and Emma dug in her purse for her cell phone. 9-1-1. Other drivers swarmed the scene, checking on victims while Emma was informed that an ambulance was en route.

She clicked off and felt a poke near her side.

"Say one word and this knife goes through you. I'll gut you right on this street."

Knife.

In front of her, neon red bounced off the building across the street and a police cruiser came to a stop just feet away. *Scream.* Emma opened her mouth.

"Not a word," the man repeated and his voice. *It's him.*

"Move," Alex Belson said. "Toward the garage. After following you for days, I almost gave up when I saw Zac. I got a bonus with that accident."

He tugged the back of her coat and she drove her feet into the ground. The pressure of that knife on her back increased. "I got nothing to lose by killing you right here. And when I'm done with you, I visit your mother."

Emma started walking. At most, she had two minutes until they reached the garage. If they got there, she was dead. This she knew. *Never let them take you to a second location.* Wasn't that what all the safety experts always said?

No second location.

She'd have to run before they reached the garage, except he detoured away from the entrance.

She pointed. "The garage is—"

"Shut up."

Emma slowed, but Alex pressed her forward, nearly shoving her. She swung her gaze left and right, searching for a weapon. Lamppost. Garbage can bolted to the sidewalk. Fire hydrant.

Nothing useful.

Then she saw the sidewalk separate and her limbs turned cold, freezing, like icicles attached to her body. She halted and Alex laughed. Monster.

If he took her into that alley, she'd be dead. No question.

"Why…why are you doing this?"

"Because you won't go away. Subtle doesn't seem to work for you. What the hell is it with you women? I speak, but you don't listen."

What? She looked at him and he pressed the

knife into her coat far enough that she felt the tip. Sharp. Deadly.

"Don't look at me," he said. "Eyes forward."

Across the street, two women came out of their car, hunched against the cold and strode in the opposite direction.

"Don't even try it," Alex said.

Emma's eyes went back to the mouth of the alley twenty yards ahead. *You're dead.*

"Please don't do this. I'll stop. I promise."

"Too late. I thought that idiot Leeks would do it, but you're just that damn fearless."

"You sent him?"

Again, he laughed, a guy simply enjoying a chat with his companion. "No. That's the beauty of it. He wanted your boyfriend to lay off his kid. Imbecile was helping me and didn't even know it."

So confused.

"The kid's a waste of space anyway. I loved her and he's an abusive psycho she couldn't stay away from. Stupid women. All of you."

"Chelsea?"

"And then I had to suck up to make sure I drew the damn case. Unbelievable. My life went to hell the minute I saw her. All I wanted was a damn report from her father and there she was, waiting for him to finish up. After that, it was over for me. Nothing but trouble."

They reached the alley. Emma stopped, threw all her weight into not moving. If she went into that alley, she'd never come out.

But Alex was bigger and stronger and he had that knife digging into her side. "Home sweet home, Emma."

Fight.

He shoved her hard enough to send her stumbling into the dark alley. Quickly, she bolted upright thinking fast. Weapon. Elbows, fists, legs. All she had. Water splashed—*he's coming*—and she whirled on him. Swung back into the general direction of his throat. Missed.

"Now she wants to play," he said in that voice, evil and menacing, that cut through her worse than any knife. "We can make this as hard as you want, Emma."

She ran into the alley, her feet slamming against the pavement. *Don't be a dead end.* Blackness surrounded her and her eyes slowly adjusted as she sloshed against the wet ground. *Oooff*—he tackled her. Her knees hit the ground first and she turned her head before doing a face plant. Her left cheek took the impact and pain exploded.

Hair tug. *Ow.* Straddling her from behind, he wrapped his hand tightly around her ponytail and yanked her head back, exposing her throat. Using his free hand, he looped something around her neck—*no, no, no.*

Emma kicked out, tried to get him off her. Too heavy. The cord tightened, sliced into the minimal flesh at her throat and she gasped.

"Crazy bitch. I set your damn house on fire and you still won't give up."

He jerked the cord tighter and tighter still. *Get him off.* She flung her arm back. Nothing there. Except the pressure released. *Free.* Emma howled, her throat convulsing from the effort of her scream and the air blowing through it. The weight on her back disappeared. She flipped over, scrambled to her feet. Extra person. Too dark to see. Both on the ground.

"Son of a bitch." Zac's voice.

"He's got a knife!" Emma yelled.

Zac pounced before Alex got fully to his feet. He shoved him, forced him to the ground. Punches flew, Alex's head snapped back and Emma ran toward him. *Check his hands*. But Zac flew backward when Alex slammed him with a kick to his midsection.

Find the knife. Too dark. She'd never find it. Instead, she hurled herself at Alex giving Zac time to recover.

"Emma, back!"

And then Emma got the luck that had eluded her for so long. A shaft of moonlight broke through the clouds and illuminated part of the alley. Two feet from her, a glint of steel winked.

Knife.

She ran toward it, picked it up. "Got the knife."

And Zac went crazy. Punches flying, kicks connecting, elbows swinging. All of it, a reign of terror on Alex Belson so fierce she wondered if the man would survive it. Alex doubled over and Zac slammed his elbow into his back, sending him to the ground. In a split second, Zac pounced on him, digging his knee into the center of Alex's back.

"Hands out," he said. "Let me see them."

But Alex wouldn't surrender. He bucked and Zac smacked him on the back of the head. Unable to wriggle free, Alex spread his arms flat.

Zac dropped his head, heaved a breath. "Dammit, Alex. What are you doing?"

ZAC LEANED ON the cold cement wall of the parking garage as officers loaded Alex Belson into a squad car. A truck rumbled by, that rotten egg smell of its exhaust hitting Zac, making his stomach seize. Nasty, that.

What had just happened?

A detective escorted Emma from the alley. They'd been questioned separately and would most likely be questioned again, but for now, they were done. He still didn't know what had happened to her. All he knew was that he'd looked up from the car accident and she was gone, walking away with some dude. He'd followed, keeping his mouth shut and his steps light, knowing he wouldn't allow Emma to get hurt.

Coming up next to him, Emma leaned against the building. "You okay?"

Always worried about everyone else. "Are *you* okay?"

She shrugged. "I don't know. I think he's the one. He didn't say it, but he said he loved Chelsea. Something about how she couldn't stay away from Leeks's son."

Zac nodded. "She and Leeks were on-again-off-again. Twisted relationship."

"I'm so confused. We trusted him. He let my brother go to prison. That filthy hunk of flesh wanted my brother to rot in a cell."

Zac dragged his hands over his face and suddenly her hand was on his back, rubbing in that way she did that made everything less intense. "I looked up and you were gone. If I hadn't looked up when I did, I'd have lost you, Emma. I wouldn't have known where you went. I've never been that scared."

She rested her head on his shoulder. "But you did look up. Thank you."

"I'm sorry I didn't believe you." He kissed the top of her head. "I could have lost you. How could I let that happen?"

Had there ever been a time when he'd been this uncertain? He'd always been the logical one in the family. Always making the right decision, and even when he didn't, it wasn't a big deal. No one got hurt or died. He'd simply learned from it and moved on. In his current state, if learning from his mistakes meant being without Emma, he didn't want to learn.

Her shoulder hitched against him and he looked down. Face collapsed, eyes squeezed shut. Crying.

Damn, he never wanted to see this strong, capable woman reduced to tears. Pushing himself off the wall, he wrapped her in his arms. "Sshhh, you're okay. I've got you. We'll figure it out. Somehow, we'll figure it out."

And they would. Because after this, job or no job, he wouldn't let her go.

Chapter Seventeen

The following morning Emma forced down dry toast, a relatively boring breakfast, while surrounded by the fancy marble and stainless steel of their temporary kitchen. If she broke something in this palace, it would take a year to pay for it. Her phone whistled and she punched the screen, scanning Penny's text summoning her to the criminal courthouse. In thirty minutes. Thirty minutes to shower, get dressed and face the end of rush-hour traffic.

Their lawyer truly was nuts.

At this point, with Alex Belson still being *interviewed,* the only thing Emma wanted from Penny was confirmation that Belson had killed

Chelsea Moore and that Brian would come home. That's it. The terror of the previous night would be worth it if Brian came home.

Why? Emma texted back.

Just get there.

Emma sighed.

"What is it?" Mom asked.

Emma contemplated a response. Something must have been happening with Brian. But she didn't have the heart to tell her mother that. *What if it's not good?*

They were too far gone for that. No more sheltering her mother. The load had gotten too heavy and this had to be—had to be—good news.

She met her mother's stare. "I'm not sure. She wants me down at the courthouse in half an hour."

"That's good, right?"

I hope so. "It could be nothing."

"I don't care. I'm going with you. It's time I started helping you."

Wow. How far they'd come in a week. All because of the Hennings family. Emma glanced down at the phone in her hand. Those crazy Hennings siblings. They'd drive her mad before this was done.

And yet she welcomed the madness.

Putting her thumbs to work, she texted Penny. See you soon. She dropped the phone, shoved her chair out. "Be ready in five minutes. I'm gonna take the fastest shower of my life and throw some clothes on."

"Put your hair back," Mom called as she charged down the long hallway behind Emma. "It's a mess."

Exactly twenty-six minutes later, Emma and her mother joined the back of the security line at the criminal courts building. On her tiptoes, Emma counted heads in front of her. Ten. Not as bad as usual, but they'd never make it in four minutes.

She texted Penny. A second later her phone rang. She didn't bother to look. She knew who it was. "Not my fault. I'm stuck at security."

"Here's the deal," Penny said, the words firing faster than usual. "My father, Zac and I are walking into Judge Alred's court. We've—the State's Attorney included—filed a joint emergency motion to vacate Brian's conviction and sentence."

Every word rolled into a massive ball in Emma's throat. She tried to speak, but only managed a high-pitched squeal. She spun to her mother and latched onto her arm.

Mom winced and Emma let up. "What?"

Finally, the massive ball trapping her words unfurled. "This is happening now?"

"Yes."

"Is the judge a good one?"

"He's perfection. A good guy and reasonable. Hang on… What?" A muffled sound came through the phone line. "He's ready for us. Hurry. Judge Alred's courtroom. 400."

"Wait."

Dead air. Emma jerked the phone from her ear and stared at it. *Don't get too excited.* The judge could deny it. Anything could happen.

Mom's face blanched.

Emma squeezed her mother's arm again. "It's good. They filed a motion to vacate Brian's conviction and sentence. In a little while we'll know if Brian is coming home."

"My God."

"Don't get your hopes up. You know our luck stinks."

Mom held her hands out, her eyes big and round and…well…happy. "But we've never gotten this far."

The gray-haired security guard Emma had seen several times before motioned her to the x-ray machine. "Step forward please, ma'am. Cell phone down."

She shoved her purse and phone on the belt. "Sorry."

He waved her through. "No problem."

Once through the machine, she grinned up at the guard. "My brother may come home today."

He offered a thumbs-up. "Good luck. Hopefully I won't see you here anymore."

Her mother stepped behind her, both of them grabbing their items off the belt. *This could be it.* Brian coming home.

Don't go there.

They got into the elevator, and Emma watched the numbers tick by until they reached their intended floor. Dragging her mother along, Emma dashed off the elevator, her low heels clickety-clacking against the tile floor. People cluttered the hallway, blocking her, forcing her to cut around them. *Just get there.* A door banged open and two men in suits stepped into her path. *Move.* Emma threw her arm out and angled around them. Her mother had better be keeping up. On her right, courtroom doors whizzed by. She checked numbers as she went. *Almost there.*

Courtroom 400.

She stopped and her mother plowed into Emma's back. Emma grabbed Mom's arm to keep her from falling over.

"Sorry. This is it."

She stared at the double doors, rocked onto the balls of her feet. "You ready?"

Mom breathed in. "I have to be."

"We've got this, Mom."

Emma swung one of the doors open, ushered her mother inside and eased the door shut. The soft click echoed and she winced. *Don't piss off the judge.*

She spun around, her gaze landing smack on the judge, a man appearing to be in his late forties. He sat behind the bench, two fingers pressed against his meaty cheek. His face gave away nothing. Not a scowl, not a smile, not a frown. He simply listened, and Emma imagined that she'd go mad wondering what the heck the man was thinking.

Zac spoke from his place at the prosecutor's table, his voice, as usual, assertive. Confident. Penny and her father sat behind the defendant's table, their postures tall but not stiff. Almost relaxed, but that couldn't be. Could it?

Judge Alred focused on Emma, then her mother, the only two spectators in the room. Not wanting to cause further disturbance, Emma slid onto the nearest bench. So what if it was way in the back? She needed to sit before her legs gave way.

Her mother landed next to her and gripped her hand. This was it. Emma clung to her mother and directed her attention to the front of the room where the judge addressed Zac.

"Counselor, why is this a joint motion?"

"Your Honor, new evidence has come to light. After examining this new evidence, we determined that said new evidence changes the State's position."

Emma tapped her foot. *Yeah, yeah, we get it.* New evidence. Blah, blah, blah. Get on with it.

"Because of this new evidence," Zac continued, "the State joins in the motion to vacate and set aside."

Please, please, please. A loud whoosh filled her head, smothered the voices of Zac and the judge. She closed her eyes. Hot little stabs traveled up her arms and made her itch. *Please let him come home.* Never had she prayed so hard, but this warranted it. She wanted her brother back. Maybe she wanted a few other things, too, but Brian coming home was the priority. If that happened, they'd rebuild their lives as a family. And, if the world could be so generous, she'd be free to have her own life and maybe make Zac Hennings part of it.

That's what she wanted. Zac, her brother and her mother. With them, she almost believed anything could happen. With them, the impossible became possible.

An immense calm inched over her, slowly smothering the pinpricks her body had just endured. Her mind went quiet and a male voice sounded. The judge.

"Okay, counselors, motion granted. Defendant is ordered immediately released."

What? Emma snapped her head sideways. "What?"

Penny leapt to her feet. "Thank you, Your Honor."

Mom held her fingers to her lips before the judge yelled at them. *Wait.* Emma turned to the front again, stared at Penny's back. Beside Penny stood Mr. Hennings and the two high-fived, their faces glowing. *It's happening.* On the other side of the aisle, Zac shoved a folder in his briefcase, all serious prosecutor but chances were he was dying to smile. He'd never give his sister the satisfaction. He'd make her beg for it.

The judge rose from the bench and rounded the corner, his long robe swaying behind him as he entered his chambers. Just like that, they were done.

Brian was free.

Penny whipped around, a mile-wide grin on her face. "*Now* you can talk."

But Emma shook her head. The words *immediately released* looped in her mind, over and over and over, and she breathed in. *Don't believe it.* Not yet. Not until they told her. Then she'd allow herself to believe that finally, after endless trudging through the justice system, they'd won.

Zac closed his briefcase, and turned to her.

Their gazes held and he finally offered up a grin that sent blood racing into Emma's brain.

Penny stood in the aisle hugging Mom whose sad, wilting eyes were now gone. *My mother is back.*

Emma jumped up. Too fast. The rush made the room spin and she held on to the bench in front of her, taking it all in. The Hennings crew huddled together, father, son, daughter. Zac and his dad shook hands, slapped some backs and—they'd done it.

"Come here, girlfriend," Penny said. "Give me a hug. We won."

And Emma lost it. She held her arms in front of her as tears barreled out of her eyes. *We won.* Mouth gaping, happy sobs rocked her. Darn, she was tired. So tired.

The foursome gathered around her, their faces a mix of surprise, shock and—in Mr. Hennings's case—curiosity. Mom had her own set of waterworks going and Emma had to look away. It was all too much. All the emotion that had been shoved deep inside, brutally packed away with the lid slammed down, came bursting free and she sobbed harder.

Zac eased her mother out of the way and stepped beside Emma. He slid his arms around her and squeezed. *He's so good.* She buried her face in his chest, bawling on his suit jacket and gripping the material at his back. *Just hold on.*

"You did it," he whispered, his lips pressed against her ear. "Why are you wasting time crying when you should be on your way to get your brother?"

Emma slammed her eyes closed. *He's coming home.*

Zac ran his hand over her head. "You're okay now. Sshhh. Emma, you did it. You put your family back together."

And then she laughed, a sort of pathetic snot-filled snort that at any other time would humiliate her, but for now, none of it mattered.

She backed away from him, grabbed the lapels of his suit jacket and tugged. "Thank you."

"Hey," Penny said. "What the hell?"

Emma rolled her eyes, but the feeling she had inside, that easy, settled hum of joy, made her attempt at irritation a lost cause. "You know I'll thank you, too. He makes me giddier than you do."

"Oh, please," Penny said. "Blah, blah, blah. We have paperwork to deal with and then you need to get on the road. Go get Brian and tonight we'll have a celebration dinner."

"But you're coming with us, right? To get him?" Emma turned to her mom. "Wait. I'm sorry. Do you want it to be just us?"

Mom dabbed a tissue over her face and grinned. "The more the merrier."

"Good." She went back to Penny. "Can you come with us?"

"If you want, I'll make it happen."

"I want." She turned to Zac. "And you, too. You should be there. We should all be there when he comes out."

He bent low and kissed her, a gentle brush of

his lips, right in front of Mom and Penny and his dad and—*wow*—that's different.

Except he blew it by stopping. "A prosecutor welcoming a wrongly convicted man home. You're determined to get me fired."

She hadn't thought about that. She tugged on his jacket, only a little disappointed. Maybe more than a little. "Sorry."

"Don't be. It'll be worth it. Let's head north."

The courtroom door opened and they all turned. Detective Leeks stood in the doorway, his vile gaze slithering over them. *He shouldn't be here.* Not when he'd done so much to hurt them, to terrorize them and to steal Brian's life.

"Leeks," Zac said, but Emma threw her hand up and stepped toward him. Behind her, she sensed Zac following. "Why are you here?" he asked.

Leeks stood still, his arms now crossed over his chest. "Thought I'd take in the festivities. Guess I missed it."

Pulverizing anger blasted through Emma. Her body buzzed and the sudden urge to lash out consumed her. She halted in front of Leeks. His son hadn't even been guilty, yet he'd been willing to ruin another man's life to protect him.

She wiggled the fingers of her right hand as Leeks stood there, that disgustingly smug grin on his face, and Emma couldn't take it anymore.

Crack!

She smacked him. One solid blast and the man's head flew sideways. From somewhere behind her, Mom gasped.

"You go, girl," Penny said.

"Whoa." Zac shifted in front of Emma. "This is over, detective. You're lucky I didn't have enough to charge you with having Brian Sinclair attacked in prison."

Leeks stared up at Zac, his eyes burning, but there was nothing to be done. Not unless he planned on taking on all five of them.

"We're celebrating," Emma said. "And you don't belong here."

HOURS LATER, EMMA, her mother, Zac and Penny stood outside the prison gates waiting for Brian.

Emma leaned against the gleaming black stretch limo Zac's father had provided and tilted her head to the sun. Spring, at least for today, had finally blessed them with its presence. All in all, a great day to welcome Brian home. Still, she had to admit, this was a scenario she'd never imagined.

Off to the right, Penny paced the edge of the parking area, talking on her phone. Mom stood by the gate, sometimes wandering back a few steps, but then returning, waiting for her baby to come to her.

Zac watched it all, occasionally checking his watch and sighing. For once, Emma didn't mind the wait. Not when anticipating the moment her brother would be free offered such excitement.

"There's one thing I'm wondering," Emma said.

Zac clucked his tongue. "Only one?"

"Hardy-har. A comedian now. Why did that nasty Detective Leeks threaten me? If his son was innocent, why did he care? I should have asked him that before I slugged him."

Zac gave her a thumbs-up. "That was a heck of a shot."

"He deserved it. I still wonder, though."

"I think he either wasn't sure his kid was innocent, or he knew the investigation had been screwed up and he didn't want their name dragged into it. Maybe both."

"I guess. It makes me sad for the Moore family. We all trusted Alex Belson. They trusted him for very different reasons, but we were all traumatized. I hope that creep never gets out."

"He'll go away for a long time. Between the murder, obstruction of justice, what he did to you, arson, and the litany of other charges my office will come up with, he'll be an old man if he ever gets out."

A buzz sounded and Emma glanced up. Inside the fence, her brother stepped out of the building, flanked by two guards. Emma's pulse kicked. Brian wore baggy jeans and a wrinkled, button-down shirt—the clothes he'd been arrested in that were now a size too big. He held a bag in his hands, most likely his personal effects. From where she stood, Emma couldn't see if his bruises had healed. Who was she kidding? Even if they'd faded, eagle-eye Mom would probably notice and Emma would finally have to explain. Later. Much later.

He's coming home. Emma placed her hands over her mouth and looked up at Zac. "I can't believe it."

"Believe it." He put an arm around her and squeezed. "Emma Sinclair, I think you're the love of my life."

"You *think?* Charming, *Zachary.* Charming."

"I do what I can." He turned toward her, rested one arm on top of the limo. "I should thank you. At the beginning of this, I was bent on proving that your brother was a murderer. I had it all figured out. He did it and I was gonna be the guy to prove it. Except nothing was what I thought. I had to experience that. Plus, I got to meet you. Something tells me that will change my life in the best way possible. I don't want to freak you out, but now that this case is history, I'll be all over you. Just so you know."

"Is that supposed to scare me?"

"Nope. Keeping you updated."

She tugged on his jacket, went on tiptoes and kissed him quick. "Excellent. And just so *you* know, I will be an eager participant as it relates to your affections."

"Glad we got that clarified."

Another buzz sounded and Emma faced front as the long steel gate slid open. Her brother stopped and looked at each guard, waiting for permission to leave. Apparently, he was stunned by the morning's activities. One of the guards set his hand on Brian's back, gave him a smile and shoved him through the gate.

The guards, like most people, were fond of Brian.

And then, for the first time in eighteen months, her brother stepped out of the prison gate. He stood there, on freedom's side of the entrance, staring at the pavement. Emma absorbed the simple joy of seeing her brother experiencing freedom. Let it heal her. No one moved. Not even their mother. Somehow, they understood that Brian needed a moment. Finally, he pushed his shoulders back and raised his head. His gaze locked on Emma's and held. Joy fused with the pain of lost time and unfurled in her chest. For months she'd imagined this moment, imagined the hoots and hollers and yet there was only quiet. The celebration would come later, but now, in the parking lot, the prison gate behind them, there was only Emma, Brian and their mother. Together.

Finally.

They'd done it.

Mom broke the spell and ran to Brian, throwing her arms around him. She sobbed, the sound of it loud and piercing and wonderful. Emma turned into Zac's side and buried her head in his shoulder.

Zac kissed the top of her head. "You did it."

Head still buried, she nodded. "He's coming home." She straightened, looked up into Zac's blue eyes and her smile, for a change, came easy. She'd smile more now. Life would be for living again. She grabbed Zac's hand and pulled him toward the gate. "We did it. He's got his life back."

"He's not the only one."

"Yep. And you, *Zachary,* will be part of it. Are you good with that? Because you have to help me with constitutional law."

"Honey, I'm great with that. We'll be a happy, twisted family."

Family. Emma's heart banged and she slapped her hand over it. For the first time since her father had passed, she pictured a complete unit. *Her* complete unit. Zac, Mom and Brian. If she threw Penny into the mix, she'd have the sister she'd always wanted. Even if Penny was crazy. Now, with Brian free, she'd grab hold of that unit and never let go. What more could a girl want? Finally, after years of losses, she'd won.

Her luck had definitely changed.

* * * * *